ABOUT THIS BOOK

AN END TO PERFECT
by Suzanne Newton

Arden's perfect world begins to fall apart the day her
brother leaves home. Then her best friend, DorJo, comes
to stay with her family, and Arden sees a chance to make
her world whole again. But can Arden make DorJo stay
without losing her friendship?

A CBC-IRA *Notable Children's Book in the Field of
Social Studies*

AN END TO PERFECT

ALSO BY SUZANNE NEWTON

M. V. Sexton Speaking
I Will Call It Georgie's Blues
A Place Between

AN END TO PERFECT

BY
SUZANNE NEWTON

PUFFIN BOOKS

PUFFIN BOOKS

Viking Penguin Inc., 40 West 23rd Street, New York, New York 10010, U.S.A.
Penguin Books Ltd, Harmondsworth, Middlesex, England
Penguin Books Australia Ltd, Ringwood, Victoria, Australia
Penguin Books Canada Limited, 2801 John Street, Markham, Ontario, Canada L3R 1B4
Penguin Books (N.Z.) Ltd, 182–190 Wairau Road, Auckland 10, New Zealand

First published by Viking Penguin Inc. 1984
Published in Puffin Books 1986
Copyright © Suzanne Newton, 1984
All rights reserved
Printed in U.S.A. by The Book Press, Brattleboro, Vermont
Set in Electra

Library of Congress Cataloging in Publication Data
Newton, Suzanne.   An end to perfect.
Summary: A twelve-year-old's seemingly perfect life
changes when her older brother decides to leave home
and her best friend has increasingly serious family problems.
[1. Friendship—Fiction]   I. Title.
PZ7.N4875En   1986   [Fic]   85-43419   ISBN 0-14-032229-9

For the Longview Writers,
especially Peggy

AN END TO PERFECT

CHAPTER 1

IT WAS ONE OF THE BEST DAYS ARDEN COULD REMEMBER. RIGHT after school they stopped at DorJo's house long enough to get her Swiss Army knife and two buckets. Then the two of them headed down to the marshes at the south end of Haverlee to look for cattails. They were in a silly mood, it being Friday.

On a whim, Arden turned an empty bucket upside down over her head so that its rim rested on her shoulders.

"Hey, Dor! Look!" she shouted, satisfied at the way the words blasted back at her from inside the bucket helmet. She could only see DorJo's legs from the knees down, but she heard her answering laughter. DorJo donned her bucket, too. They walked along yelling back and forth, singing snatches of songs and listening to each other's strange, robot voices.

The dirt road they took was a cut through someone's farmland. On one side was a soybean field, on the other a pasture surrounded by rail fence. They did not see Seth Fox coming along behind them on the pasture side of the fence, walking as fast as he could to catch up.

Suddenly DorJo stubbed her toe on a grass clump growing in the middle of the road. Arden saw her friend's legs stagger and stumble in a vain effort to regain balance. Then DorJo's bucket clanked and rolled on the road right underfoot, too close for Arden to do anything but fall over it. As she went down, her bucket head fell off, bounced once, and lay still. The two of them sprawled in the dirt, about to die laughing, too tickled to do anything but point at each other and shriek.

So when Seth just appeared out of nowhere and said seriously that he thought he ought to go with them to help carry the buckets of cattails, it was just one more funny thing. Seth was the smallest person in the entire sixth grade, even smaller than Arden. Beside DorJo's sturdy five feet seven inches, he looked like a grasshopper, thin and reedy. She could mush him with one hand if she wanted to.

"Listen, Seth Fox," DorJo said, half-laughing, half-serious, "the day I let you tote something for me will be the day Jesus comes again! Go find something else to do. We don't want you along." She got to her feet, slapping the dust from her jeans.

Seth stayed where he was. Perhaps the rail fence that separated him from the girls gave him courage. His wary blue eyes were shaded by pale lashes. His sun-bleached white hair lay thin and flat on his head, so that to Arden he looked like some kind of little ghost boy.

"Arden don't care if I go," he persisted. "Do you, Arden?"

She, too, stood up and picked up her fallen bucket. "Dor and I told Mrs. Baucom we were going to get the cattails for the fall dried arrangement at school," she said. "We don't need anybody else." Even as she said it she felt a shade guilty. She didn't like to hurt anyone's feelings.

"You can't keep me from going if I want to," Seth said with

4

unexpected pluck. "It's a free country. I can follow you anywhere you go and you can't do anything about it."

DorJo put her hands on her hips and stared at him with exaggerated disbelief. "Say what, now?"

Uncertainty crept into his voice. "You heard me."

"Yeah," said DorJo. She moved menacingly toward the fence. "I sure do *think* I heard you. But maybe I better get a little bit closer just to be sure I didn't misunderstand your words."

Seth began to back away. Arden noticed how bony he looked under the thin T-shirt. He must be crazy to stand up to DorJo Huggins like that, or else he wanted to go cattail hunting mighty bad.

DorJo strode to the fence, planted her two hands on the top rail, and in the next instant had vaulted over into the pasture. Seth did not wait to see what she would do next. One thing for sure—Arden thought as he sped away—he certainly was light on his feet. He must have air in his bones!

DorJo shook her head at his retreating figure. She never moved to pursue him, just watched him run to the far end of the pasture and fling himself over the fence on that side. Then he stood up and saw she hadn't chased him.

"You just wait!" he hollered, all out of breath. "You're gonna be sorry!"

"You're already sorry!" she called back, laughing. She turned her back on him and climbed over to Arden's side of the fence.

"Maybe we should've let him go along," Arden said. "He's not so bad, as boys go."

"Are you kidding?" DorJo picked up the other bucket and they resumed their walk. She gave an impatient swipe at her short black hair, which tended to hang in chunks and strings. "I've got no patience with boys—always bragging about how fast they are, or how strong. Shoot! There's not a one in the

5

sixth grade I couldn't beat up with one hand tied behind my back. Can you see that little pip-squeak Seth Fox totin' a bucket for *me*?"

"Well," said Arden, "that might've been an excuse. I guess he wanted to be along for the fun."

"Let him go find his fun somewhere else," said DorJo. Arden knew that tone of voice. It meant "case closed."

She smiled to herself, thinking how much all the sixth graders held her friend in awe. DorJo wouldn't let anyone call her by her real name, Dorothy JoAnna. It was her own idea to put them together into one stark, tough-sounding name. She was strictly a no-frills person, but around Arden she sometimes showed a softer side that others never saw.

"It sure is a pretty day, isn't it?" Arden said dreamily, tilting her head back to gaze at the cloudless sky. It was one of those perfect late-September days, when the browns and tans of dying foliage caught the sun's glint and turned the countryside into gold. Days such as this she felt like reaching out both arms and hugging Haverlee close to her. Sometimes she felt as though she were living in a magic kingdom. Perhaps it had an ending somewhere behind the trees that lined the horizon, but she had no interest in what lay beyond the trees—everything she loved most was right here.

"You look funny when you walk along with your nose pointed at the sky," DorJo said. "You're liable to trip if you don't watch out."

Arden laughed, thinking about the two of them falling all over the road back there.

"You ought to wear your hair undone," DorJo went on critically. "If *I* had curly blond hair, *I* sure wouldn't wear it in pigtails."

It was a very un-DorJo-like thing to say. Arden looked at

her, mildly curious at the turn the conversation was taking. "It's too long and frowsy. It would get in my way."

"I guess you wish Seth *did* come along, don't you?" DorJo asked.

"No, not especially. It's more fun with just us. I guess I mostly feel sorry for him."

"Well, then, why didn't you holler at him to come on back if you wanted him to go so bad?" DorJo's tone was belligerent.

"Dor, can't you hear? What did I just tell you?"

DorJo's jawline stiffened. "How come you hang around with me anyhow?" she said, ignoring Arden's question.

"Are you trying to get rid of me or something?" Arden asked.

"No!" In the pleasant round face DorJo's brown eyes were gloomy.

Puzzled, Arden went over the day in her mind, trying to think what could be the matter. It had been just a regular Friday, hot in the classroom and smelling of sweaty bodies and old paper. She and DorJo occupied the two middle-row front desks, right under Mrs. Baucom's nose. It was DorJo's idea to go get the cattails, and Arden was glad enough to go along, since no one in her family would be home before five. Mrs. Baucom had promised to take Arden's books by the house and leave a note that she'd be home by dinnertime. That was it. For the life of her, she couldn't think of a single thing that had happened to explain DorJo's present mood.

"Did I do something to make you mad?" she asked.

"No, you didn't do anything to make me mad," DorJo grumped. "I just want to know why you hang around with me, is all!"

"Because I *like* you, dummy! Do you think I'd waste my good time with somebody I didn't like?"

DorJo did not seem convinced. "Aw, you like everybody."

She swung her bucket hard, back and forth. Its handle squeaked in protest.

"What brought this on?" Arden asked. "We were doing fine, having fun and laughing, and now you're growling at me like I was Seth Fox or somebody!"

DorJo did not reply. She strode a step ahead so that Arden had to walk faster to keep up. It wasn't until she made a loud, sniffling noise that Arden realized her friend was crying. She couldn't remember ever seeing DorJo actually cry before.

"Gosh, Dor—what *is* the matter!" She reached out and clutched at her friend's arm. They had come to the patch of woods that led down to the creek where the marshes were. There were no good sitting places, so Arden upended her bucket and sat on it.

"I'm not going another step till you tell me what this is all about," she said stubbornly. "You might as well fix your bucket and sit!"

At first DorJo hesitated, but then she turned her bucket up and sat on it. She wiped her eyes with the back of her hand. Arden reached into her own shirt pocket and pulled out a rumpled tissue.

"Here," she said. "Don't look at it too close."

DorJo stalled for a while, dabbing at tears and blowing her nose. She acted embarrassed.

"Whatever I've done, I wish you'd tell me so I could quit doing it," Arden told her.

"You ain't done anything," DorJo said in a subdued voice. Then with a great sigh she added, "Well, you might as well know—Mama came back home last night. When you and I went by the house a while ago, she must've been asleep in the back room."

"Oh," said Arden, understanding right away. DorJo's mama was not exactly what a person would call regular-on-the-job.

She had been gone for several months now, since late spring, in fact. Nor was it the first time she had left DorJo and her older sister Jessie alone in the little rental house on Purdue Street. DorJo and Jessie had pretty much taken care of themselves for the past three years. Jessie was seventeen. She had dropped out of school last year to work full time at the chicken-processing plant.

"I was going to tell you when you came by for me this morning on the way to school," said DorJo. "Only, I just had a hard time making the words come out. Then I thought that since we were going by my house for the knife and buckets, you'd see her for yourself and I wouldn't have to tell you. Only, she was asleep." Her voice trailed off. She gave Arden a look that was somewhere between ashamed and defensive.

"Well," said Arden carefully, "I guess you're glad she's back, huh?"

"It was real late when she came," DorJo said, not answering the question. "I was already in bed. Jessie got off work at eleven o'clock and had only been home about fifteen minutes when there was this noise at the door and in Mama walked with a big bag of groceries and all kinds of sweet words. She didn't knock or nothing. She acted like she'd only left that morning and we weren't supposed to notice she'd been gone."

Arden tried to imagine what it would be like if Mom went away for months and came home suddenly like that. But Mom was not anything like DorJo's mother. "Well . . . did you hug her, or what?"

"She wanted us to sit around and talk. Jessie said she didn't feel like it—she just went to bed. So it was me and Mama."

"So . . . what did you talk about? Did she tell you where she'd been, or anything?"

"No. That's the part we're supposed to pretend—that she's

never been anywhere but right here. Jessie won't pretend, though."

"What about you?" Arden asked.

DorJo looked away. She rubbed her left fist with her right hand. "I know she's been gone," she said after a moment. "But I won't talk about it if she don't want me to. I don't want to make her mad."

"What did you talk about, then?"

"School. She asked me how I was doing. I told her I was making pretty good grades this year with your help, and she said—"

DorJo stopped. The next part seemed to stick in her throat like a sideways fishbone.

"She said . . . ?" Arden prompted.

"She said you prob'ly felt sorry for me. She said you only hung around with me because I'm so much bigger than everybody else and you like the protection. She said I should watch out—you'd throw me over for somebody that was richer and smarter—"

Arden sprang up so quickly the galvanized bucket tipped and rolled a little way. "That makes me so mad!" she said through clenched teeth. "What does she know? She stays gone all the time! What right does she have to say those things about you and me when she's not even here to see for herself? Talk about throwing somebody over—gosh, *I've* been here the whole time she's been gone, the old . . . the old—"

Suddenly she realized that she was raving about DorJo's mother. "I'm sorry," she said lamely. "I didn't mean to talk ugly about her, but I hate what she said. It's a lie. You're the best friend I ever had. I never felt sorry for you a single minute, and I guess if I need protection I have a perfectly good dad, not to mention a brother in high school and a mother who knows karate!"

The gloom in DorJo's expression began to lift a little. "You act like you really mean that."

"Of course I mean it!" she was yelling again. "What have I got to do to prove it—jump off the Empire State Building or something?"

DorJo grinned sheepishly. "No," she said, "I guess not. I believe you." She stood up then, and picked up her bucket and Arden's, too. It was her way of apologizing for calling their friendship into question.

They walked down the sloping path through the cool woods in comfortable silence. As they neared the creek, the ground underfoot became mushy. The air smelled of insects and water, mud and decay. It was a curious smell, right on the verge of being objectionable.

"The best cattails are usually over this way," DorJo said, picking her way through tall grasses around the water's edge. Arden followed cautiously. Horseflies buzzed around their heads. Clouds of fuzzybills rose from the grasses and whirled and danced about them. She felt she dared not breathe too deep or they'd go up her nose and into her lungs. Maybe they'd lay eggs in there, and the eggs would hatch.

They came at last to the spot where the cattails grew thickest. Dozens of them poked up from the placid shallow waters like cigars on sticks. Some of them had already burst and sent their cotton-cloud seeds away in the wind. They were like the old sofa on Belle Thomas's back porch, the one with the stuffing coming out and scattering all over the yard.

"How're we going to get them without getting our feet wet?" she asked.

"There's no way to do that unless you know how to fly," DorJo said. "You can go in barefoot or with your shoes on. Or you can stand there and let me get them."

Arden looked down at her sneakers. They weren't exactly

brand-new, but she wondered what Mom would think when she came home with them soaked in creek water. On the other hand, the idea of padding about in the ooze barefoot, not knowing what she might step on—places like this were full of snakes and frogs and snapping turtles.

"Sneakers," she said. "I didn't come all this way to watch you have all the fun."

They rolled up the legs of their jeans and waded in. Arden gritted her teeth against the unnatural feeling of water seeping into her shoes, but in a minute or two she got used to it. DorJo got out her prized possession, the Swiss Army knife that Jessie had given her for Christmas last year. It had cost a lot, but DorJo made good use of it on their excursions around Haverlee. Now, while Arden held the stalks, DorJo sawed away at them until they broke in two. It was quite a trick to harvest the cattails without making the brown covers start to shed.

Neither of them talked much while they gathered the reeds. Arden found herself keeping an eye out for anything moving. She tried not to think about what might be in the mud under her sneakers. By the time they had enough cattails to fill both buckets, the sun was getting low.

"I hope Mrs. Baucom didn't forget to go by and leave my books at the house," Arden said as they waded out of the creek, "or my folks won't know where I am."

"We'll be back in about twenty minutes," DorJo said, "if we walk fast."

Arden eyed her soaked shoes. They felt awful, all slick and gooshy. Maybe walking would squeeze some of the extra water out of them, but right now drops splattered with every step she took.

She picked up her bucket, noting that it was not only heavy, but that the long cattails made it hang from her hand at a tipping angle. For a split second she regretted that they hadn't let Seth come along to help carry the full buckets. But she would never say that to DorJo.

They started back up the path, squishing as they walked and laughing at the strange noises their shoes made. Arden was in front, holding her bucket out to the side so that it wouldn't bang against her legs.

Suddenly, between one second and the next, she was falling forward, so fast she had no breath to cry out before she lay sprawled on the path, her bucket lying out of reach, the cattails scattered. She felt very stupid. She had no notion of how she had gotten there—she hadn't stubbed her toe or anything.

"Arden! Are you all right?" DorJo said at her back.

"I guess so." She pushed herself up and then stood, wiping halfheartedly at the dirt on her jeans. "That was weird! I must be accident prone."

"Ha! That wasn't a accident," DorJo exclaimed. "Look there!"

Arden's eyes followed her friend's pointing finger. Stretched across the path about ten inches above the ground was a piece of copper wire, barely visible in the muted forest colors. It was tied around the trunks of two small pines on opposite sides of the path.

"Doggone that Seth!" DorJo snorted. "What a stupid trick. Don't he know I'll cream him at school tomorrow?"

"Do you really think Seth would do something like this?" said Arden. "Little old *Seth*?"

"Well, who else would—"

They looked at each other. The quiet woods were no longer friendly. DorJo's eyes seemed unusually wide and dark; Arden felt sure that hers did, too. Up until now her greatest fear had been snakes. She swallowed. A little old snake might be a pretty welcome sight right now, compared to some other things a person might run into.

CHAPTER 2

"WELL," SAID DORJO IN A LOUDER-THAN-NECESSARY VOICE, "LET'S get these cattails picked up and go on home. Your dad's liable to be here any minute looking for you."

Arden was too tongue-tied to respond. She and DorJo scrambled for the cattails scattered on the ground. She hoped fervently that whoever had strung up the wire hadn't heard her remark about her folks not knowing where she was. No need to help the enemy more than necessary.

"Cut the wire just before we start off," said Arden, close to DorJo's ear.

"No. I don't want them to know I've got a knife," DorJo whispered.

They put the cattails back in the bucket and kept going. Arden hoped she looked as unruffled as DorJo did. The path out of the woods seemed much longer than when they had come down it an hour or so before. They were more cautious now, training their eyes on the ground ahead in case there were other booby traps. Arden grabbed up a long, broken-off limb beside the path. She shifted the unwieldy bucket to her left hand and held the limb at an angle ahead of her, like a metal detector.

"This way we can tell if there's a wire before we get tripped," she said. "Besides, I can hit somebody with it if I have to."

Suddenly, from almost directly overhead, the air was shattered with peals of laughter. No—it was more like the giggling of a maniac. Arden and DorJo looked up. There, among the stout limbs of a live-oak tree, sat Seth Fox and Albert Twiggs.

Albert was an eighth grader, huge for his age, but more plump than muscular. He and his mother fancied him to be brilliant. Others in Haverlee were more likely to describe him as lazy, although not to his face. His size made him more or less immune to insult from anyone smaller or younger. DorJo, however, had gotten away with it once when she told him— in front of a bunch of eighth graders—that he needed to go on a diet. When he started after her, she outran him, proving her point. Since that time he had not been fond of DorJo.

Now he was obviously pleased with himself, out of reach as he and Seth were from the girls. Seth, for his part, looked merely uncomfortable.

Arden's fear rapidly turned to anger. "You nerds!" she yelled. "What do you think you're doing?"

"Sitting here in this tree," Albert said in a voice that was beginning to deepen. "Enjoying the songs of the birds and the . . . er . . . other scenery. There is a great deal of interesting scenery. For example, a short while ago we saw a flat-chested, blond-crested Ard-bird take an unexpected tumble—"

"Shut up, you dingbat!" DorJo said tersely.

"What if we don't want to shut up?" Seth spoke up. "It's a free country—what're you gonna do about it?"

"You sound like a broke record," DorJo said in disgust. She

mimicked him: " 'It's a free country!' Is that the only thing you know? What good is a free country to a little twerp like you? If they was to give it to you on a silver plate with parsley around it, you wouldn't know what to do with it!"

Her words had a grandness about them that demanded an equally grand response. Seth was not capable. His mouth worked as he tried to think of something scathing to say. He couldn't even find anything to throw at them.

"I think it's going to make a pretty good story in school Monday morning," Albert said. "How the invincible DorJo Huggins, Terror of Haverlee, and her sidekick, Arden Gifford, were scared out of their wits on the afternoon of Friday last in the woods."

"Yeah!" echoed Seth, as though *he* had said the words.

Arden wanted to take the cattails and leave. What difference did it make what kind of dumb stories those two told? "Come on," she said to DorJo. "I'm getting bored."

"Yeah, me too," DorJo said. "But first I'm going to do something to unbore myself."

"Like what?"

DorJo took out her Swiss Army knife and opened several of its thirteen blades. She pulled a hair from her head and tested the sharpness. Arden watched the boys in the tree. DorJo had captured their interest, all right. Seth involuntarily pulled his dangling legs up to the limb on which he was sitting.

"Good idea, Seth," Arden said in her best tough voice. "I wouldn't make myself any bigger target than I had to, if I were you."

"Aw, she ain't gonna do nothing with that knife," he said.

"Listen," said Albert. "We could come down out of the tree and get that knife away from you so fast you wouldn't know what hit you!"

"Yeah!" said Seth.

"Is that so?" DorJo was cool. She held the knife balanced flat on her palm. "Well, why don't you just come right on, then, and we'll see if you're right?"

Enjoyable as the scene was to Arden, she couldn't help noticing that the light was fading. The sun was just above the trees now. They couldn't stay here all night, keeping the boys treed.

"Arden," said DorJo, "why don't you just start looking around for dried grass and pine straw and pinecones and things? We'll pile them around the base of the tree."

"Are you crazy?" Albert tried to sneer, but he wasn't too successful. "Do you think for one minute that you can scare me? Do you want to serve twenty years in prison for starting a forest fire, dummy?"

"Oh, I won't have to serve a term," DorJo said. "There won't be no witnesses."

"What about Arden?" Seth's voice was high and thin. "*She's* a witness."

"Friends don't testify against each other," DorJo said with a grin.

Arden set down her bucket and began to gather the pine straw and cones as DorJo had directed. She knew very well it was all a joke. If these dumb boys had a grain of sense, they'd know it, too, but the knife had scared them, so they weren't thinking straight.

In about five minutes she had gathered a respectable pile around the base of the tree, amused by the continuing bluster from the boys overhead. She stood back, dusting her hands, to admire her work.

"Yep," she said, "I guess this makes me an accessory."

"A *what*?" DorJo said.

"It means she's guilty, too," Albert the know-it-all called down from the tree.

"Shut up—nobody asked you anything!" DorJo said. She reached into her jeans pocket with her left hand and pulled out a tiny box of matches. She kept the knife steady in her right hand. "Okay, Arden, take this box of matches here, and when I give the signal, you light the pile."

"Right." Arden took the matches. Neither of the boys could see DorJo's broad wink. "I think I have a couple of scraps of paper in my pocket, too. That should speed things up."

Without warning, Albert's heavy body came crashing down through the branches and landed in front of them. Arden stumbled back, expecting him to leap at DorJo and wrestle the knife from her hand. Instead, he took off up the path, never looking back for an instant, never saying a word.

In the silence that followed his departure, the two girls looked up at Seth, deserted, on the tree limb. Arden thought she'd never seen anyone look so scared. She almost felt sorry for him, but then, he'd gotten himself into this mess.

"If I was you," DorJo said to him softly, "I'd do a better job of choosing my friends. Some of 'em just don't have any staying power."

Seth made no reply. His face had lost all color. He stared, fascinated, at the match in Arden's hand.

"Come on," DorJo said in her most commanding voice, "get down out of the tree."

Seth did not move.

"Come on. It's getting late."

"Put the knife up." Seth's voice was dry and raspy, as though smoke was already rising to choke him.

DorJo shrugged and closed the blades. She tucked the knife back into her pocket and, with one contemptuous foot, scattered the piles of dry wood and cones that Arden had placed around the tree.

"Here are the matches." Arden handed them back.

Seth came down then, wincing when twigs poked him through his thin shirt.

"I don't know what you had in mind," DorJo scolded as he descended, "but Arden's the one that fell because of your stupid trick. Nobody but a coward would pick on her when they was really mad at me."

"Y'all are buddies, ain't you?" Seth said, breathing hard from his exertions. He seemed gratified to have his two feet on the ground again. "You stick together like two fingers on the same hand. It's no way a person could do something to one without gettin' mixed up with the other."

His head was slightly bent as he spoke, as though he fully expected DorJo to level him then and there.

Arden stepped between them. "You're right," she said. "We're together in everything. Maybe your 'friend' Albert Twiggs has a different idea about it, but—"

"He ain't my friend," Seth mumbled, his eyes still downcast.

"*That's* pretty clear!" DorJo snorted.

"You might as well go on," Arden said, dismissing him. "Only, I think you'd better cut that piece of wire before somebody trips over it and breaks their neck."

"I got nothing to cut it with," he said.

DorJo reached into her pocket and handed him the knife. "Here. Use this."

It was a tense moment. Seth struggled within himself. Then, without a word, he turned on his heel and went down the path to the place where the wire was strung across the path. In a couple of minutes he was back. He handed the knife to DorJo.

"That's sure a good knife," he said.

"Yeah, Jessie gave it to me for Christmas."

There was a moment of awkwardness, and then Arden picked up her bucket of cattails. DorJo did, too, and they started up the path. Arden could hear Seth's footsteps following close behind them, but no one said anything.

When they came out of the woods onto the road, Seth said, "I can help carry the buckets."

"Like I said this afternoon, I don't need your help carrying no bucket!" DorJo snapped.

"I never said you needed help." Seth raised his voice. "I know you don't *need* it, but it ain't gonna hurt you. Besides, Arden might want some help."

DorJo's pride was sorely tested by the argument. Arden tried to think what she could do to put the best face on things. It wouldn't be right for Seth to carry just her bucket and not DorJo's.

"I have an idea," she said.

"It better be a good one," DorJo grumbled. "Some people sure know how to mess up a perfectly good day!"

Arden chose to ignore the remark. "Seth can walk between us and hold on to both handles. That way it won't be hard on anybody."

DorJo didn't reply, but when Seth stepped between them she shifted her bucket to the left hand so that he could grab hold. A few steps along she said, "This is like three camels trying to go in different directions. We got to get in step or we're gonna drop every one of these cattails on the road. When I say 'Left' get on your left foot."

Arden and Seth obeyed orders, shuffling their feet around until the left one came down on the correct beat. It felt good, marching along in rhythm and in step, swinging the two buckets of cattails like parade banners between them. The painted sky silhouetted the trees on the horizon, like The End at the close of a good movie. They walked all the way to DorJo's, set the two buckets on the side porch, and parted ways just as the September twilight descended.

CHAPTER 3

ARDEN WAS STILL SORTING OUT THE PIECES OF THE DAY WHEN she walked into the kitchen, so Mom's first sharp words took her by surprise.

"Arden Gifford, where in the world have you been?"

She blinked and Mom came into focus—red sweater dress, blue apron, hands on hips, half-relieved, half-exasperated.

"With DorJo at the creek gathering cattails," she said. "Mrs. Baucom promised she'd come by and leave my books and a note so you wouldn't worry. Did she forget?"

"No—I found them on the porch when I got home. But it's nearly seven o'clock, Arden!"

"Well, we would've been back sooner, but . . ." she paused, wondering how much to tell. ". . . but I stumbled and dropped my bucket. We had to pick up all the cattails. And the buckets were heavy—we had to rest a lot coming back." She studied Mom's face as she talked, to see if she was persuasive enough. The hands came off the hips.

"All right," Mom said. "Just don't do it again. You girls

shouldn't be wandering around by the creek alone. You might have fallen in, and how would I have known?"

Arden didn't reply to that. Mothers always thought of the worst possible thing that could happen. "Did you save me any supper?" she asked timidly. "I don't care if it's cold."

Mom's face relaxed into a smile. "In the oven. Milk's in the fridge."

Arden washed her hands at the sink, staring dreamily out of the window at the expanse of dark blue sky. A few stars winked at her. The moon's near-whiteness was unnaturally beautiful. She was certain that the twilight sky appeared in this way only to the people of the Kingdom of Haverlee, but because they had been here forever they—

"What happened to your shoes?" Mom interrupted her thoughts. "They look a little the worse for wear."

She had forgotten all about the wet sneakers, having become used to the way they felt. "I didn't want to step in the creek barefooted."

"So you waded in with your sneakers on?"

"Yes'm." She got her full plate out of the oven and took it to the table, hardly able to meet Mom's eyes.

"Well, I guess it's a good thing you didn't wear your Sunday best today." Mom sighed.

"Are you mad at me?" Arden asked. She pulled out the chair and sat down.

Mom gave her a mock-hopeless look, then laughed. "Well, I'll admit that when you weren't home by six I *did* rehearse a few stinging lines about being responsible and all that, but—"

"But what?"

"But I used to be twelve. I can't be too self-righteous."

Arden grinned. Mom untied the blue apron.

"I have a meeting with a couple of school-board members

tonight. After you wash your dishes you'd better take a bath and start your homework. Oh—and throw those wet sneakers in the washer tonight, so they'll have time to get good and dry before Monday morning."

"Yes'm," said Arden. Mom went out, leaving an impression of herself in the room. The best thing about her, Arden thought, was her sense of humor. Sometimes she brought home funny stories from her job at the Porterfield hospital, where she worked as a medical technician. Arden liked the way she saw the light side of serious things.

Hill was in the upstairs hallway when Arden went to take her bath. "Hello, Aardvark," he said. "Where were you? Mama got pretty antsy when you didn't show up for dinner."

"DorJo and I were at the creek, looking for cattails."

"Find any?" he asked, although he didn't seem really interested in the answer. There was something restless about Hill lately, something she couldn't quite put her finger on.

"Sure—all we could carry. It was fun."

He grinned at her with real affection. He looked more like Dad every day with his dark wavy hair and the dimple in his left cheek. The high school girls thought he was cute. They spoke to her because she was his sister. They asked her questions about him. At first she wondered whether they expected her to tell Hill how interested in him they were, but in the end she decided to keep it to herself. She didn't like being used as a go-between. A few of them made a habit of hanging around McDonald's, where he worked most afternoons and Saturdays.

"Ah, to be twelve again!" he said with a dramatic air, as though he were as old as Methuselah. "When life was uncomplicated—"

"Oh, for pete's sake!" she said, disgusted. "You don't have to make fun—"

"I'm not making fun, Aardvark," he said. Something in his voice made her look at him more closely. In spite of the teasing he seemed sad somehow.

Maybe that's what happened when you got to be seventeen. A person heard a lot about "the teens." It sounded as though some spell was cast over people when they turned thirteen, so that they gradually became ugly and hard to live with even if they'd never been that way before. Everybody expected it to happen, grown-ups and kids alike. Arden rather dreaded it, knowing full well that she couldn't prevent herself from becoming a teenager when the time came. Thank goodness she had only just turned twelve! Being one of the younger people in the sixth grade did have its advantages. Still, she took some encouragement from the fact that Hill had never been ugly and hard to live with. She wished she could cheer him up.

"What's the matter?" she asked.

"Nothing's the matter." He gave her a playful punch on the arm as he passed her to go downstairs.

But a little while later, when she came back down with the marshy sneakers in hand, she heard Hill talking to Dad in the living room.

". . . driving me nuts," Hill was saying. "I told you and Mom I'd try it. Well, I have. It's not going to work. School's been going on for three weeks now and it's getting worse instead of better. I'm so bored I daydream in class all the time. I can't help it."

Dad didn't respond right away. Arden could imagine him sitting in the brown leather chair, stroking his chin and looking at Hill while he thought of what to say.

"Have you really given it your best shot?" he asked at last. "Independent study projects and that sort of thing?"

"The whole bit, just the way we talked about it last spring. I've done everything the teachers have suggested and some

24

extra besides, but there are times I think I know more than they do about some subjects. I need calculus. I need four years of foreign language. I'm wasting my time if I stay here two more years."

"Well, then," Dad said with a sigh, "I suppose we'd better start looking for a solution to the problem."

Arden hurried to the kitchen, walking as softly as possible. She put the sneakers into the washing machine and poured in the detergent, but then thought better of turning the switch to On.

How could Hill be bored in Haverlee? There was so much to do!

". . . with Gran and Big Dad," she heard Hill say when she returned to her listening place in the hall. "I could live with them in Grierson and go to Pressley High School—it's one of the best in the state. I'd be a big help around the house—I could do stuff for them that they can't do anymore."

. Dad chuckled. "I'd like to be there to hear you suggest to Gran and Big Dad that there are things they can't do. You'll have to be more diplomatic than that or you'll never get to first base."

"Whatever!" Hill said impatiently. "They'll be glad to have me."

"That's probably true, on one level," Dad agreed. "But having a grandson visit and having him as a permanent resident are two different things. They'd feel like full-time parents again."

"Couldn't we at least ask them?" Hill pleaded. "How about if we go tomorrow and talk to them about it?"

"I suppose we could," Dad said reluctantly. "I'll talk it over with your mother when she gets home from her meeting. She doesn't like the idea of your leaving home, I can tell you that."

I don't either, Arden thought indignantly. How could Dad even consider such a thing? She felt like storming into the living room to tell them so, but that would be dumb.

"Gran and Big Dad should have an out," Dad reminded Hill. "Big Dad has just retired and Gran isn't teaching. They've been making big plans about things they're going to do now. They shouldn't feel guilty if they don't really want to take responsibility for you. They have a right to say no."

"Sure, I know that."

"Let's think about another alternative—a backup plan."

Arden could tell by the silence that Hill hadn't been thinking of other plans. "Well," he said after a few moments, "we can't afford a prep school."

"You'd better think about it between now and tomorrow," said Dad.

"O.K." Hill sounded discouraged. "I've got to go now—I promised Kathy I'd pick her up at eight fifteen."

"Sure—have a good time. Don't stay out too late."

Arden ducked back into the kitchen and turned on the washing machine. She couldn't bear the thought of Hill's leaving. The house would be so empty without him. What could she do to make him want to stay?

She went to the kitchen window and watched as he backed his VW out of the driveway. The moon had moved until it was no longer framed in the window. The night seemed much darker. Suddenly she didn't want to be by herself. She snapped off the light and went into the living room. Dad was leaning back in the brown reclining chair, staring up at the ceiling.

"Hey, Bird," he said when she came in. "I haven't seen you all day."

"That's what you get for going to work before I could get down to breakfast," she said, planting a kiss on his forehead. "If EZ Appliances' plant managers didn't have to go to work so early, they might get to see their children grow up!"

He laughed outright. "You may have a point there—although you know I'm here for breakfast most days. Pull up a seat and I'll watch you grow right now."

"You looked as though you were thinking about something," she said carefully, pulling the footstool close to his chair.

"Well, yes, I was."

She waited to see whether he would volunteer information. She didn't want to confess to eavesdropping unless she had to.

"Can you tell me?"

He turned his head sideways to look at her. "I suppose so. Your brother wants to leave home."

Even though she knew it, she felt the shock anew. The words were so blunt and to the point. Tears stung her eyes.

"It's not that he doesn't like us anymore," Dad went on, keeping his eyes on her face. "Hill's just too smart for Haverlee. He needs a bigger school, more college-prep courses. We have to help him find a place."

"Where?"

"He wants to go live in Grierson with Gran and Big Dad. If they can't see their way clear to take him, he'll have to think of something—some*one* else." His eyebrows went up. "Do you have any good ideas?"

"Why would he want to go to Grierson to live anyhow?" she said grumpily. "I think it's an awful town!"

Dad looked surprised. "Hey, wait a minute! You're talking about my hometown. I lived there most of my life, before your mom and I were married."

"Well," she said, "I love Gran and Big Dad, but I don't like Grierson."

"I didn't know you felt that way about it," he said, interested. "I thought you liked those long visits with Gran and Big Dad— going to the movies, the park, the library—all those things you could never do here in Haverlee. Have you always disliked it?"

She thought about it before she answered. It was true that when she was younger she liked the town very much. The stores were exciting. There was always something to do, somewhere to go. There were parades and carnivals, the circus once a year, museums, and concerts.

"I don't like the people."

Dad's brow furrowed ever so slightly. "Oh? Which people?"

She traced the seam on the side of her pajama leg with one finger. How could she tell him about the way she was treated by the girls Gran invited to play with her? Gran had taught many of them in second grade. Probably their mothers and fathers had been Dad's friends when he was a little boy. When Arden went to visit, Gran always called up someone for lunch and play. Years ago it had been fun—they'd played dress-up in Gran's old clothes, had tea parties under the magnolia tree in the front yard, or taken pretend trips in the summer-house glider. But this past year had been different. The girls who came over—Becky and Kim, Teresa and Liz—treated her as though she were not quite worth associating with. She had the feeling that they quarreled with their mothers about coming. They didn't want to play anything—in fact, the word "play" seemed to offend them. Mostly they wanted to talk about boys and clothes. They wore makeup and high-heeled clogs. When she was around them, Arden felt like a weed among orchids, or worse, like a baby.

"All of them," she said, sidestepping the question. "They're stuck-up."

"Well," Dad said, "I had no idea."

"I don't know exactly how to explain it," she said. "It's like they're acting out parts instead of being themselves. They talk like TV people. Regular people are . . . are plainer than that."

Dad gave her a sort of one-sided smile. "There may be something to what you say," he allowed. "Sometimes city people tend to act more . . . sophisticated. Of course, it may have more to do with the particular people you've met in Grierson. I expect there are some of the plainer variety around."

She shrugged. It was of no importance to her, really. Hill was the one who wanted to live there. He had a different view of the place than she did. "I wish he wouldn't go." She sighed. "Couldn't you forbid it?"

Dad reached over and gave her a big hug. "No, I'm afraid not. *I* don't want him to leave, either, but Hill is a very bright young man. It would be downright criminal to make him stay in Haverlee when he wants and needs to be in a better school."

"But," she said, "what if Gran and Big Dad say no?"

Dad frowned and leaned back again, searching the ceiling as though he thought the answer might be up there. "I've been thinking about it."

"Mom's going to say no," Arden said confidently.

Dad looked over at her. "We've talked it over before. She'll probably say yes."

"Why've you kept it a secret from me?" she asked. "You've talked about it for ages and never let me know."

"Well, we didn't want to worry you about something that might never happen. I thought we could work it out so he wouldn't mind staying here until he graduated. I suppose your mom and I want him to stay so badly we haven't really taken him as seriously as we should've."

They sat in silence for a few minutes. Then she asked, "When will he go?"

"Soon. I don't believe he wants to get too far behind in the school year."

"You mean, maybe by the end of this month?"

He nodded. "Or the first of October."

She didn't even want to think about it. "I have to do my homework," she said, standing up. "G'night."

" 'Night, Bird." He kissed her cheek. "Say, we may have to drive to Grierson tomorrow to talk with Gran and Big Dad. How do you feel about going along?"

One part of her wanted to make excuses, but she realized that this was kind of a family crisis. The least she could do for Hill would be to go along and see how things turned out.

"All right. I'll go."

"Good for you! See you in the morning."

She worked late, doing row after row of arithmetic problems and a whole page of sentences for grammar. Their orderliness comforted her. She worked until she was too sleepy to think, and then went to bed. She dreamed that she and DorJo and Seth were marching back to Haverlee with their buckets, but when they came to the outskirts, the town had disappeared.

CHAPTER 4

HILL DROVE AND DAD SAT WITH HIM IN THE FRONT SEAT. ARDEN and Mom were in the back seat.

"You remember when Arden and I would ask 'How many more miles is it?' " said Hill.

"Yes—usually when we'd been on the road about two minutes," Dad said. "Then one of you would ask every two minutes from then until we got to the city limits of Grierson. It's the most boring question in the world!"

"Yeah," said Hill, "and it has a lot of boring answers, too—sixty miles. Fifty-nine miles. Fifty-eight miles. Little kids don't even know what that means."

"Then why do they ask?" Mom wanted to know.

"I just wanted some assurance that we were really moving," Hill said. "It seemed that we were standing still, it took so long to get there."

Not for me, Arden thought. At least, not anymore. I'd be happy if we never got there. She looked out the window at the familiar scenery. Somewhere between Haverlee and Grierson there was a point where she usually lost interest in what was out there and started reading a book. This time she decided to pay attention all the way to Grierson, to see if she could discover the exact spot where the land was no longer interesting to her.

She loved the flat terrain and the thick growth of trees, the rich dark earth and the expanse of sky where she lived. The closer they came to Grierson, the redder the soil became. The land was hilly and full of rocks, the farms terraced with curving furrows. The houses seemed to sit starkly on top of hills, with few trees for shade. The harsh bareness bothered her. No wonder these folks fled to towns! The boundaries of her magic kingdom lay somewhere along this highway, between the dark earth and the red.

"You're awfully quiet today, Arden," Mom said.

Arden turned away from the window reluctantly. Suppose she missed the spot she was looking for because she was not paying attention?

"I don't have anything to say."

"How do you feel about Hill coming to live with Gran and Big Dad?"

Arden quickly turned to look out of the window again. She shrugged. "It's all right, if that's what he wants to do."

"Won't you miss me, Aardvark?" Hill asked. She heard the teasing in his voice. It made her mad.

"*Yes*, I'll miss you, but I don't expect that'll make you change your mind about going, will it?"

She hadn't meant to yell, but she was very close to crying. People had no business teasing about serious things. Everyone got very quiet.

"Sorry," Hill said gently. "I'm going to miss you, too."

Oh, shut up! Arden thought. The lump in her throat grew

bigger by the second. The tears in her eyes and nose threatened to spill and disgrace her.

"No need to talk so big!" she said crossly. "You may not be leaving, you know!"

More silence. She had the feeling that everyone's attention was focused on her, and she hated it. She wished she hadn't come along.

Dad leaned over and switched on the car radio, to fill the space with neutral sounds. He and Hill argued a little over which station. Arden leaned her forehead against the window and took up her vigil again.

Even so, she missed the point of change. She realized, all of a sudden, that the landscape was different. The scarcity of trees, the red color of the soil, the rocky ground—it had happened, and she hadn't seen exactly where. Maybe she hadn't been concentrating hard enough.

She turned to Mom, who was looking out of the other window. "Where does it change?" she asked.

Only when she saw the bewildered look on Mom's face did she realize that the question wasn't connected to anything outside her own thoughts.

"The land is different here," Arden said. "Where does it change?"

"Oh," Mom said. "Well, you know Haverlee is in the coastal plain. This is the Piedmont—the hills. North Carolina has three very distinct geographic regions—a coastal plain, the foothills, and mountain ranges as well."

"I wasn't asking for a geography lesson," Arden said. "I just want to know where it changes!"

Now, that doesn't sound like me, she thought, dismayed at the impatience in her tone. She wasn't angry at Mom, and yet it sounded as though she was. She could tell by the look on Mom's face that her feelings were hurt.

"I was about to say," Mom said, "that the coastal plain used to be the floor of the ocean up until less than a hundred thousand years ago. That accounts for the flat terrain around Haverlee. At the point where that prehistoric ocean ended, the land rises rather abruptly. It's called the fall line. I'm not sure exactly where the rise begins, but I expect there are maps that show where the waterline was. Naturally, the soil content is different."

Oh, thought Arden, turning back to look with new eyes at the landscape. Once my kingdom was underwater. No wonder it was different from this land! She imagined herself eons ago strolling along the ocean floor in a pale green light, looking upward at the diffuse rays shining downward through the moving water. Maybe in another life she had been a great finny beast gliding through the deep, and coming to the hills made her feel like . . . like . . .

"A fish out of water," she said aloud, and then promptly regretted it.

"Who's a fish out of water?" Hill asked from the driver's seat. "Me?"

"I think Hill will do just fine in Grierson," Mom said, completely misunderstanding. "Before long he'll be at the head of his class—and he'll have plenty of friends, too."

"I wasn't thinking about Hill when I said that!" She wished people would quit trying to read her mind. They were wrong every time.

The conversation turned to how they would approach Gran and Big Dad, how it wouldn't be tactful to bring up the subject until they had visited a while. Signs advertising Grierson businesses began to crop up along the roadside. Soon they were at the city limits, and already surrounded by exhaust fumes and town noises—clanging and roaring, hissing, puttering,

34

screeching. She could not hear a single bird song or the voice of a person. Arden felt trapped. It was all she could do not to put her hands over her ears and shut her eyes tight.

By the time they turned the familiar corner to Talley Street, Arden's very bones hummed. Gran and Big Dad lived in a large, two-story white house, square as a box and trimmed with dark green. The huge magnolia in the front yard had been planted by Dad and Uncle Bob when they were little kids. It was a family joke that blades of grass forced their way through the cracks in the front walkway, but no grass would grow in the magnolia's shade.

"Just goes to prove," Big Dad would say, "that magnolia shade is more powerful than cement. Don't know why the public works department doesn't catch on and pave our streets with magnolia shade!" He said it at least once every time they all got together, and people laughed every time.

Arden was weary of all the predictable things the members of her family did and said to each other. In light of the changes that were about to be made, old words seemed stale and inappropriate.

They piled out of the car into the gravel driveway, and Big Dad came out as he always did, looking like a huge old bear in plaid Bermuda shorts with his hat pulled down over his balding head. His pear-shaped body extended from narrow shoulders outward over paunch and hips and back in to skinny legs. Gran followed, wiping her hands on her apron. She was a tiny person, as light on her feet as someone half her age. Her gray hair was short and trim, and her face was bright and smiling.

They are like a picture, Arden thought, looking at them and the house as though she had never seen them before. They are picture-book grandparents in a picture-book house.

Through all of the hugging and exchange of pleasantries,

no one seemed to notice that Arden withheld herself. That suited her fine. When the rest of them gravitated toward the house, she wandered around to the backyard on the pretext of looking at the fall flowers and stayed there until Gran called her in to dinner.

Gran's dinners were a spectacle. This one featured baked hen and rice with thick giblet gravy, homemade rolls, fresh fruit salad, beet pickles, butter beans, stewed corn, and a lot of other things that Gran kept bringing out to the round oak table. Arden had no trouble devouring what was set before her. Gran's cooking was one thing that she hoped would never change. Not until they were all served a mound of homemade ice cream on a slab of pound cake did the purpose of the visit come up in conversation.

"Well," Big Dad said in his bass voice, "you sounded mighty mysterious over the phone, Tom. What's up?"

"Well," Dad said, "Hill has a proposition to put before you and Mother."

"Oh, I see." Big Dad's amiable gaze turned to Hill. Arden didn't think she had ever seen her brother so nervous. "What is it, fella?"

Hill wiped his mouth with the large linen napkin and put both hands in his lap. He looked as though he was supposed to recite the pledge of allegiance and had forgotten the first two words.

"Well, first of all, I want you and Gran to feel free to say no," he began.

Big Dad nodded. "That goes without saying. When a person gets to be my age, 'no' is one of the more basic words in the vocabulary."

"Now, Jake!" said Gran, giving him a light slap on the wrist. "Quit teasing! Go on, son. Don't pay any attention to him."

Hill took a deep breath and plunged in. Big Dad's large

36

blunt fingers tapped impatiently on the white tablecloth, but he didn't interrupt. Gran's head was tilted to one side. Arden had the feeling they'd already guessed what was coming.

"I wouldn't expect you to wait on me or anything like that," he finished. "I'd wash my own clothes and my own dishes, and I'd—"

Big Dad held up a hand. "Hold on there, boy! You don't have to promise your life away."

Hill fell silent. Arden could see the pulse beating in his neck under his shirt collar.

"So," said Gran, "you want to live with us and go to school here?"

"Yes, ma'am." He looked agitated. Arden wished that Gran and Big Dad would look a little more pleased about the idea. They seemed very cautious.

Then she thought, Whose side am I on, anyhow?

"Being a teenager in Grierson is quite different from being one in Haverlee," Gran said worriedly. "Especially nowadays. I'd die if anything happened to you while you were here with us."

"I don't remember your being that nervous when Bob and I were Hill's age," Dad said.

"Hmph! You don't have any idea how much I worried. But it's different when it's your child's child—that makes you feel doubly responsible. Times have changed. There are so many more temptations for young people now than when *you* were young."

Arden scraped the bottom of the ice cream dish and wondered if she dared ask for a second helping. The conversation made it sound as though teenagehood really *was* an affliction from which no one was safe. Also, Gran implied that a person might have a worse case in Grierson than in Haverlee. Arden could well believe it—the extra noise alone would be enough to aggravate any ailment a person might have.

"Well," said Gran, "Jake and I need to talk it over. We may not be able to give you an answer today, Hill."

"Oh, that's all right." Hill tried not to look disappointed. "I didn't expect you to answer right away."

It fell to the three females to do the washing up after dinner. Gran was of the old school—she thought that women should put away food and wash dishes while the men went somewhere to talk about important things. Mom, on the other hand, felt that women had matters to talk about that were just as important. At home Dad and Hill had kitchen duty as much as Arden and Mom did, and Arden had to learn how to do home repairs and mow the lawn, the same as Hill.

Arden's job was to dry Gran's best china and silver carefully, so that it wouldn't spot. She listened to the conversation between Mom and Gran. A person could find out lots of things by being quiet and appearing not to be at all interested.

"One thing I do hope," Mom said, clanking the plates in the sink harder than was good for them, "is that if Hill comes to stay, you won't wait on him hand and foot. He knows how to run the washer, he's a good cook, and he can keep a straight room if he thinks anyone's going to come around checking."

"Well," Gran said noncommittally, "we'll cross that bridge when we come to it." That was her way of saying "No promises." Gran was kind of set in her ways. Arden figured it would be just as hard for her *not* to wait on Hill as it would be for Mom to do it. Gran's attitude was "You run your household your way, I'll run my household mine." That would be true even if part of Mom's household went to live with Gran.

"You're not saying much today, Arden," Gran said. "I don't think I've ever known you to be so quiet."

Arden gave a little shrug. She lined up the silver knives in a gleaming row on the kitchen counter.

"Don't you care whether Hill comes here to live?"

Arden glanced up in time to see the warning look from Mom. Mom expected her to flare up like she'd done this morning in the car.

"I'll miss him," Arden said in a steady voice. "I wish he didn't have to leave Haverlee. But if that's what he wants to do, it's all right with me."

"Well, that seems to me to be a very grown-up attitude," Gran said briskly, drying her hands on a towel. "Now—you two go about your business and let me see if I can corral Jake into discussing this matter right now. No need for poor Hill to be left in suspense any more than we can help."

"I think I'll go lie down for a few minutes," Mom said, stifling a yawn. "That dinner made me sleepy. How about you, Arden?"

She made a face. Afternoon naps were kid stuff.

"How about if I call Liz over?" Gran said, reaching for the telephone. "She probably—"

"No!" said Arden. "I mean, no ma'am. I . . . I'd rather not, this time."

"Oh, well, suit yourself," Gran said, heading for the back door. "I just don't want you to be bored."

Arden went out to the front porch and sat in a rocking chair, propping her feet on the railing. How she wished DorJo were here! She wondered whether Gran and DorJo would like each other. Her friend was certainly different from Liz and Teresa and the other town girls Gran invited over. DorJo would love this house—Arden could already imagine her exclaiming over the funny clothes and the old-fashioned toys in the attic junk room. Maybe if Hill *did* come to stay, she and DorJo could come to visit him some weekend. They could sleep in the big blue bedroom and talk way into the night. Grierson might not be so bad with DorJo here.

The screen door opened suddenly and Hill came out. He seemed surprised and not especially pleased to see that she was already occupying the porch.

"Have they decided yet?" she asked.

"No. They're out in the backyard, talking." He straddled the porch railing and leaned against the post. He jingled the coins in his pocket and whistled through this teeth.

"What will you do if they say no?"

"Stay in Haverlee, I suppose." He sounded glum. It made her feel sad.

"I hope they say yes," she said quietly. He turned to look at her.

"Really?" he said. "You seemed awfully angry about it this morning. I thought maybe you might be just a tad jealous."

"Jealous! You mean because you're leaving Haverlee and I'm not? Boy, are *you* ever off base! I never want to leave Haverlee as long as I live!"

"O.K., O.K. So I was wrong!"

"I like our family the way it is," she said. "You and Mom and Dad and I. It doesn't seem right for you to go away, but I guess I can get used to it."

"Sure you can. After all, I'd be leaving for college anyway in a couple of years. And you, too, eventually. You won't always want to live there."

"Ha! That's all *you* know," she said loftily. They might have gotten into an argument then and there, except that Dad came out on the porch.

"Gran and Big Dad want to talk to us, Hill," he said. "They're in the living room. Arden, would you run upstairs and wake your mother?"

She got up slowly from the rocking chair and went to carry out the order. She hated to wake Mom up, especially for this.

Mom was in the blue room, fast asleep on the great four-poster bed with its satin comforter and ruffled pillow slips. Arden had always felt it was a bed fit for royalty. Whenever she came to spend the night, this was her bed.

She touched Mom's arm, carefully, so as not to startle her. "Mom? Are you awake?"

Mom stirred and opened her eyes. She had that where-am-I look a person gets when they're awakened in a strange place. "Oh, hi!" she said sleepily, her eyes focusing on Arden. "Is it time to go home already?"

"No—Gran and Big Dad want you downstairs."

Mom got up quickly then. She reached for her purse on the night table and took out her comb. "Goodness!" she yawned. "I could've slept for another hour."

"Are we going home right after they tell us what they've decided?" Arden asked, going to stand beside Mom in front of the huge dresser mirror. They didn't look much alike. Mom's dark hair was short and neat. She had a straight little nose and friendly brown eyes that could see right through a person. Arden's blond braids hung down behind her, and the little hairs frizzed around her forehead like the blooms of a smoke bush. Her eyes were more green than brown, and her expression was very sober right this minute.

"Well," said Mom, running the comb through her hair, "I suppose it depends on what they've decided. If they say no, there won't be anything else to talk about, at least for today. Hill wouldn't want to hang around—it's hard not to show when you're disappointed. On the other hand, if they say yes, we may have to stay quite a bit longer working out the details. As Gran would say, let's cross that bridge when we come to it."

"Am I supposed to go to this meeting, too?" Arden asked as they started down.

"Well, of course. Don't you want to know what's going to happen?"

Arden didn't answer right away. She did want to know, but she wasn't at all sure she wanted to hear it firsthand. She didn't know what her face would do. Mom didn't seem to expect an answer. She put her arm around Arden's shoulders and gave her a little squeeze. "Do what you think is best," she said. "I'd like to have you around, but if it's too hard to take, then you don't have to be there."

Arden leaned against her. It was good to have somebody who understood how she felt.

When they came into the living room, the other four were already there—Dad and Hill on the dark green sofa, Big Dad in his saggy corduroy lounge chair, and Gran perched on the edge of one of her antique straight chairs like a bird about to fly. Arden felt she could almost reach out and touch the tightness in the air.

Big Dad cleared his throat. "I guess we can get started now."

"Sorry," Mom said. "I was asleep." She sat between Hill and Dad. Arden didn't want to be where anyone could look at her. She moved to a corner out of the way.

"Sally and I've talked this thing over from all the angles we could think of," Big Dad began. "The first thing I want to say, Hill, is that we're honored you'd even ask to live with us— most kids your age would rather do anything than live with their old-fogy grandparents."

"But you're not old-fogies," Hill said.

"That's true," said Big Dad, "but I'm pleased that you recognize it. Shows how mature you are."

Dad snickered and Mom giggled. Big Dad gave them a look that said "Behave yourselves."

"I hope you don't think, just because we didn't jump up and down and clap for joy, that you aren't welcome here. Sally and I have been making plans—some traveling we've been wanting to do, some friends we've been wanting to have come for a long visit. We had to think through what difference it would make if you were here."

Hill leaned forward, gripping his knees. Arden could tell that he was trying hard to keep his mouth shut.

"What we decided," Gran broke in, "was to go right ahead with our planning and let you work around it. Once you get settled here in school you'll make friends, I'm sure. If we have to be away several weeks, no doubt you can find someone who'd be willing to let you stay with them."

"And," said Big Dad, "we'd expect you to do your share around here. I know you have responsibilities at home—you'd have them here, too. Also, we'll have to work out some rules . . . about curfew and car driving and all. Your mom and dad allow you to do some things that may make me feel uneasy. You might just have to accommodate to our ways until we get over being nervous about having a teenager in the house again."

"Does this mean . . . yes?" Hill seemed almost afraid to believe it.

"Yes," said Big Dad with a broad grin.

Hill leaped to his feet, ran across the room, and gave Big Dad a huge hug. Then he picked Gran up and swung her around. "Gosh, thanks, you two! I promise I'll be so wonderful you'll wonder how you lived without me!"

Everybody roared with laughter, even Arden. All the tightness in the air dissolved, and the planning began.

Later, as they drove home in the twilight, Hill was higher than an unstrung kite. He babbled on until Arden wanted to stuff her fingers in her ears. She was glad that he was happy, but enough was enough. There ought to be at least a moment of silence for the mourners.

CHAPTER 5

ON MONDAY MORNING ARDEN TOOK A SHORTCUT THROUGH BELLE Thomas's backyard and arrived under DorJo's kitchen window at exactly 8:35, according to the Timex she had just inherited from Hill. It had a wide vinyl band and a round face with black numerals, just the kind she preferred. She did not like digital watches, with their numbers pulsing under glass like little frog hearts.

Dad had taken the whole family out to dinner in Porterfield after church yesterday, and they had spent all afternoon there. When they got back it was nearly dark. Mom said it was too late for her to run over to DorJo's, so Arden had to be content with making a long list of things she had to tell her, including Hill's leaving in about two weeks. Now she felt as though she would absolutely pop if she and DorJo didn't get to talk soon.

"DorJo, I'm here!" She didn't say it very loud, for fear of waking Jessie. DorJo was usually just inside the kitchen door ready to go.

She waited a moment, and when her friend did not appear, she called again. Still there was no response. She moved closer to the side porch and listened. Last year DorJo had overslept only once on a school morning, and that was because she had been sick the night before. Maybe she was sick again. Maybe getting her feet wet in the creek had given her a sore throat. Thinking of the creek made Arden remember the cattails, and she looked at the spot where they had left the two buckets on Friday. They were gone. Here and there, though, she saw tufts of the airy seeds, evidence that some of the cattails had come apart.

Frowning slightly, she tiptoed up the wooden steps onto the porch.

"DorJo?" she said again, very close to the bedroom window. Nothing stirred. She listened hard, but there was no sound at all from inside.

DorJo wouldn't have gone to school without her. Months ago they had made a pact never to leave each other without advance notice. Besides, the two bucketsful of cattails were too heavy and unwieldy for one person to carry. She turned and rapped sharply on the side door.

"For God's sake!" shouted a female voice from somewhere in the house. "Shut up that noise and let a person sleep!"

Horrified, Arden nearly fell backward off the porch. The voice did not belong to either DorJo or Jessie. For a crazy instant she thought she must have come to the wrong house. Embarrassed, she tumbled down the wooden steps on spaghetti legs and ran across the yard into the road. She ran until she was out of breath, her book pack bouncing against her back like a limp papoose.

She stopped at last because her side hurt, and a little bit of sanity returned as she gulped air. It was then she remembered what DorJo had told her Friday about her mother's return. Of course—the voice had to belong to Mrs. Huggins. But where was DorJo? And Jessie?

All the way to school she paused every now and then to look back, hoping against hope that DorJo would be coming along behind her. She couldn't imagine why her friend would leave without her, but she knew DorJo would have a good reason.

She climbed the eight sagging steps to the west entrance of the school. Mrs. Baucom's was the first room to the right, and she was already seated at her desk working. No one else was in the room. Arden saw at a glance that DorJo's desktop was exactly as she had left it Friday afternoon.

"Hello, Arden!" Mrs. Baucom looked up and smiled. Not a strand of her wavy gray hair was out of place. Her blue dress made her look calm and serene. Arden felt better instantly.

"Hello," she said. She slipped the book pack from her shoulders and set it on her own desk. "Mrs. Baucom, has DorJo been in this morning?"

"Why, no. In fact, I was surprised to see you come in alone. I know you usually walk together."

"She wasn't in her house when I went by." Arden could not keep the tremor out of her voice. "Somebody was—but not DorJo."

Mrs. Baucom put down the pen she had been writing with. She put both hands flat upon the desk, as though she intended to push herself up. "Oh? What do you mean?"

"I called a few times, and no one answered. Just as I was about to go, I knocked once, and a person yelled at me. It wasn't Jessie. Maybe—well, it could have been their mother—" She stopped. Perhaps Mrs. Baucom didn't know about DorJo's mother. Maybe DorJo didn't *want* her to know.

"Are you worried?" Mrs. Baucom asked in a kindly way.

"Yes'm," Arden said.

"Well, I'll tell you what. If DorJo hasn't arrived by the time the bell rings, I'll send word to Mr. Cranston."

"We went to get cattails on Friday," Arden told her. "We had two bucketsful and we left them on DorJo's porch. They were gone this morning."

"Probably she moved them for some reason. Try not to worry."

The other students began to arrive. Three buses drove into the school parking lot almost at the same instant. Through the open window Arden could see Mr. Cranston directing the unloading. She liked him. He knew everyone's name in the whole school. Sometimes he came to their classroom and sat in the back row. He did the work with the rest of the class, and sometimes he raised his hand to answer a question. His answers weren't always correct, and then everyone would laugh. Mr. Cranston didn't mind—he laughed, too. As long as Arden had gone to Haverlee School, he had visited the classes.

Seth Fox walked into the room, the single strap of his homemade denim book bag digging into his left shoulder. Arden was glad to see him and smiled. Self-consciously he put his books on his desk and strolled over to where she sat.

"Where are the cattails?" he asked, first thing.

"I don't know," said Arden. "I don't know where DorJo is, either."

"What do you mean?"

"She wasn't home this morning and she hasn't come to school. The cattails are gone from where we put them Friday night."

The bell rang sharply and Mrs. Baucom rose from her chair, the signal for everyone to get to their desks as quickly as possible. Arden saw by Seth's expression that he was as mystified as she was.

Mrs. Baucom's eyes scanned the room until everyone was

settled. "I see that Billy Wayne and DorJo Huggins are absent. Does anyone know about either of them?"

"Billy's got asthma!" said a voice from the back of the room.

"Ask Arden about DorJo," said Nina Wall. "She ought to know."

"She don't!" Seth said emphatically, turning in his seat to challenge Nina.

"Well, you don't have to yell at me!" Nina bristled.

"That's enough, now," said Mrs. Baucom. She bent to make marks on a paper. Arden watched, feeling sad. So far this year, DorJo hadn't been absent. She wanted to get a perfect attendance prize, the same as last year. If she didn't show up before the middle of the day, her chances were gone for good, and it was only the beginning of the fourth week of school.

Mrs. Baucom went through the usual morning routine, collecting lunch money, making announcements. After what seemed a very long time, she called Arden to the desk and handed her a folded piece of paper with Mr. Cranston's name on it. The absentee slip was stapled onto it. "You may take this to Mr. Cranston," she said.

"Is it about DorJo?" Arden whispered.

The teacher nodded, but she didn't tell Arden what was in the note.

Maybe, she thought, as she went along the hallway to the principal's office, he will let me go look for her.

Ms. Keys, the school secretary, was collecting lunch money and attendance reports from all the classes. There was quite a line. Arden was careful to let people ahead of her, so that she would be the last. When she got to the desk, Ms. Keys reached out her hand for the report, scarcely looking to see who had brought it.

Arden did not put the papers into Ms. Keys's hand. The

secretary looked up from the sheet she was writing on and wiggled her fingers impatiently.

"Hello, Arden. I'll take that."

"I have to see Mr. Cranston." Her heart was beating somewhere at the base of her throat. It made her chest hurt. "This note is for him."

"Let me see it," Ms. Keys commanded, reaching for the papers. For one brief second Arden considered holding it out of her reach, but then she gave in. It wouldn't be excusable. Ms. Keys removed the staple and set the attendance report aside while she read the note. Arden scanned her face to see what it might tell her, but Ms. Keys had been a principal's secretary for a long time. Her eyes and expression reflected nothing.

"Mr. Cranston has someone with him right now," she said. "Why don't you run along to your class?"

She didn't say "like a good little girl," but it sounded to Arden as though she meant that. Something in her tightened and held.

"Because it's pretty important," she said, trying to keep her voice steady and polite.

Ms. Keys's face became suddenly stiff. "Well, I really don't know when he'll be able to see you. He's very busy."

Arden locked eyes with the woman for a long moment. She wanted to say 'This is more important, whether you know it or not!' but insolence wouldn't help DorJo's cause. She glanced at Mr. Cranston's inner office door, shut tight. Perhaps he wasn't really in there. Maybe he had gone fishing and left a dummy of himself sitting in the big swivel chair behind the desk.

"Run along, now," Ms. Keys said again, no longer trying to hide her irritation.

"Would you mind telling me what the note says?" Arden

asked. It was a terribly bold and hopeless thing to do, but DorJo was her best friend. You had to do whatever you could for a best friend.

"I really don't think it's any of your business," Ms. Keys said. "The note was addressed to Mr. Cranston."

"Well," said Arden recklessly, "*you* read it!"

Ms. Keys's eyes flashed. "Arden, go back to class! I don't have time—"

At that moment the inner office door opened and Mr. Cranston came out. Arden peered past him into the office. She didn't see anyone at all.

"Hello, Arden," said Mr. Cranston, smiling kindly.

"Hello, Mr. Cranston," she said. "Could I please talk with you for just a minute?" She didn't dare look at Ms. Keys.

"Well, of course!" he said. "Come into my office."

"Here," said Ms. Keys sullenly, handing him the note. "You'd better read this."

"Thank you," he said. He took it with him into the office. "Have a seat there by the desk, Arden."

She sat down and then watched as he read the note. His curly hair was untidy in a nice way. He already looked tired, even though it was just Monday morning. He looked at the note a long time, frowning as he read.

"All right," he said finally. "What did you want to see me about?"

So he wasn't going to tell her what the note said. Well, then, she'd just have to get down to business.

"I'm worried about DorJo. We always walk to school together, but this morning she wasn't at home. A person in the house yelled at me to shut up, but it wasn't DorJo or Jessie. It might have been their mother, but why wouldn't DorJo be there? I *know* she wouldn't skip school, because she wants perfect attendance. And, besides, we were supposed to bring cattails to class today so Mrs. Baucom could fix decorations for fall, and—"

"Hey, hold on there!" said Mr. Cranston, leaning forward. He smiled at her in a funny way. "Take a breath or you'll pass out."

She did take a breath then, and heard her own run-together words echoing in the room. Probably Mr. Cranston thought she was rattlebrained.

"Let me get this straight," he said. "You and DorJo always walk to school together, right?"

"Yes, sir."

"But this morning she didn't come out, even though that was the plan?"

She nodded. "And somebody yelled at me. I got scared and ran. I didn't know what to do."

"You did the right thing, I expect," Mr. Cranston said, studying her. "You say the person who yelled might have been DorJo's mother. Wouldn't you recognize her mother's voice?"

"I'm not . . . sure." Arden felt that she was stepping through a nettle thicket barefooted. "See, most times I've been over there, her mother's been . . . out." For some reason it seemed unwise to tell him that DorJo's mother's absences were longer than those of most mothers. She was the only person besides DorJo and Jessie who knew it and she felt she had no right to tell.

"Hmmm. Strange," he murmured, tapping his finger on the desk. He stared off into space. For a moment she wondered if he had forgotten she was there, then he roused himself and looked at her again. "You're pretty sure DorJo wouldn't skip school?"

"Positive. She got perfect attendance last year. She wanted it again this year, I *know*."

Mr. Cranston opened a file drawer beside his desk and

flipped through some folders. He pulled one out and looked at its contents for a while. Then he said, "They don't have a telephone."

"No, sir."

"Well," he said, looking at his watch, "I'll run over to their house and check into this."

She felt a tremendous rush of gratitude. "I really do thank you," she said.

He stood up, then, and she got up, too. They walked out together. Ms. Keys's rigid back was testimony to the fact that she was not of a forgiving spirit. Arden was careful to keep her face blank when she passed the secretary's desk. As she went down the hall toward her classroom, she wondered if Ms. Keys thought she had told on her about the lie.

At lunchtime Seth sat at her table in the cafeteria. Nina Wall made much of the fact that he was the only boy at the table.

"What're you doing here, anyhow?" she said. "We don't want any boys at our table!"

"It's a free country," Seth countered.

Arden looked sideways at him as she sipped her milk from the carton. DorJo had mocked him for saying that, and yet it seemed a good argument. It *was* a free country. Even so, it must take a lot of guts to sit at the girls' table, especially with the other boys calling out snide remarks from two tables away. She tried to imagine plunking herself down at a table full of boys. The notion made her scalp prickle. Wild horses couldn't make her do such a thing!

Seth sat unperturbed through lunch, paying no more attention to her than to any of the other girls, yet she knew very well he was there because of her. It made her feel very strange, both flattered and embarrassed. She was thankful that he didn't talk to her, because if Nina and the others started teasing her about Seth, she was afraid she'd end up being mean to him, just to save face.

All day she waited, hoping that Mr. Cranston would walk into the classroom with DorJo in tow, but no such thing happened. When the last bell rang, Arden took her time packing her books. Seth lingered by the door.

"You going home now?" Seth asked as they went down the steps.

She shook her head. "No. I have to talk to Mr. Cranston."

"I'll wait for you," he said.

"It's going to be a while," she said, looking at her Timex. "He has to get the buses loaded."

"I can wait," he told her. "My folks don't get home from work till six."

He was like one of those flies at the creek—the kind that you couldn't run away from once they got in orbit around your head. Still, she found that she was glad for his company. They sat on the steps not talking until the last bus pulled away in a flare of dust and spattering gravel. Mr. Cranston turned and saw them sitting there. Arden got to her feet and went to him.

"I just wanted to know what you found out," she said.

"Not a whole lot," Mr. Cranston said, glancing beyond her at Seth, who had also come closer.

"Seth was with DorJo and me Friday when we brought back the cattails," she said, to explain his presence.

Mr. Cranston's forehead crinkled into many little worry lines. He rubbed the side of his face with his open hand, the way people do when they're trying to decide what to do next. Arden felt suddenly uneasy.

"Arden, I'm not sure what's going on. I went to DorJo's house and spoke with Mrs. Huggins. She says that there was an . . . argument Friday night and that DorJo left the house.

She says she hasn't seen or heard from her since that time."

Arden got very still inside. She felt like she did the time she fell out of the swing and got the breath knocked out of her.

"But . . . but where would she go?" The words came out in a whisper.

"Well, I hoped you'd be able to tell me. Mrs. Huggins wasn't very helpful."

"Doesn't she even *care?*" Arden's voice rose. "Isn't she even looking for her?"

"It appears not." Mr. Cranston seemed sorry to have to tell her.

Arden looked at Seth without really seeing him, stricken suddenly with the realization that DorJo had not come directly to her in time of trouble. "Oh, gosh! She's been gone since Friday night? Mr. Cranston, this is Monday! Oh, gosh . . ."

Mr. Cranston put his hand on her shoulder. It felt strong and steady. "Arden, look at me."

She did so, trying to focus through her fear on his eyes.

"It's right for us to be concerned about DorJo, but don't start making up the worst possible things. My feeling is that she got upset about something at home and left. She must have had somewhere to go."

"But why didn't she come to my house? Where else would she go? Where is Jessie? Did you talk to Jessie? She would know—"

"Well, Jessie wasn't at home either. I'm sure that she and DorJo are safe together somewhere."

"She works the three-to-eleven shift at the chicken plant." Arden looked at her Timex. "She'd be going to work right about now. Couldn't you call the plant and talk to her?"

"I'll tell you what " said Mr. Cranston, "why don't you go home now? I'll visit the plant when I get through here at school and talk to Jessie if she's there."

"Will you call me up and tell me what she says?"

"Yes—probably around dinnertime."

Arden breathed deeply. This was like a bad dream, one of those where you need to run as fast as possible, but every movement is slow and difficult.

"If you learn something I should know about, call my house and leave a message," Mr. Cranston said.

"Yes, sir, I will." She started away, dimly aware that Seth was still there beside her like a pale shadow. He hadn't spoken a word the entire time. Now he hoisted his book bag slightly to relieve the weight on his thin shoulders. His worn sneakers crunched the gravel underfoot.

"If you want," he said, "I'll go with you to look."

"I don't know where to look," she said woodenly. All the time she was thinking, Why didn't DorJo come to me? Of course, she might have come over Saturday when we were in Grierson, or yesterday when we were at church or in Porterfield. Maybe she tried one of those times and gave up. Maybe she feels like I have deserted her.

The more she thought about it, the more wretched she felt. What good is a friend who isn't there when you need her?

"We could go to the creek," he persisted. "Maybe she went back down there."

"That snaky place?" Arden scoffed. "She'd never go there— not to stay three whole days! That's a dumb idea." Her own misery and helplessness made her speak more harshly than she intended. She wasn't mad at him but at herself.

"Well, there must be *some*place," he retorted. "Everybody has a hiding place."

She opened her mouth to argue but light broke even as she did so. She stared at him, amazed. It was true—she and DorJo did have a hiding place, a secret place known only to them. DorJo had showed it to her after they became fast friends.

Excitement welled up inside her and she began to walk faster.

She couldn't tell Seth. The hideout had been DorJo's place first. Arden swore on a tattered Bible that she would never reveal its whereabouts to any other person, not even if she were tortured. But even though she couldn't tell Seth, she felt she owed him something for the idea.

"Why do you want to help look for DorJo?" she asked him point blank. "She . . . we were kind of mean to you Friday."

He shrugged. "Well, *you're* worried . . ." His words trailed off, but they hung there for her to hear again inside her mind.

"Are you?" she asked.

"If you are." He shifted the book bag again. Arden wondered what DorJo would say if she knew that little-old-nothing Seth had offered to hunt for her.

They were almost in front of Arden's house by this time. "I'll see you tomorrow," she said as she turned to go up the walk.

Disappointment showed plainly on his face. "Aren't you going to look for her *any*?"

"I might, later on," she hedged. "If I need your help, I'll call you."

"I ain't got a telephone. You'll have to come to my house to get me."

"All right," she said. "Thanks for the offer."

She watched him trudge up the street and turn the corner, wondering again at his strange sense of loyalty. He was certainly different from the other boys she knew.

CHAPTER 6

IF DORJO HAD LEFT HOME IN A HURRY, MOST LIKELY SHE DIDN'T take any food with her, Arden reasoned. She rummaged in the refrigerator and found some cheese and an apple. From the cabinet she salvaged the last of a bag of potato chips, some crackers, a box of raisins, and a pop-top can of Vienna sausages left from Hill's last camping trip. When she couldn't find Hill's canteen, she settled for filling a quart jar with ice water. She wrapped it with a dish towel to keep it cold and to keep the other things from getting wet.

Next she took her school books and papers out of the book pack and put the food in. By the time everything was packed, it weighed more than she expected. For a brief moment she considered leaving the water jar behind, but then she remembered that people can go without food longer than they can go without water. When she left the house a few minutes later, the muffled slosh of water and the clicking ice cubes made a pleasant rhythm to walk by.

She intended to go directly to the hideout, or at least as

directly as she could without being seen—she and DorJo never went straight to the place. But the nearer she came to DorJo's house, the more she felt drawn to turn in there. What if DorJo had come home again? In spite of her dislike of Mrs. Huggins, it seemed important to Arden to find out firsthand, if she could, what had happened Friday evening.

She left the road and crossed the bare, shady yard to the little house. She smelled ham frying and heard the unmistakable sizzle of meat on a hot griddle. She made herself climb the wooden steps and knock on the side door. Her heart pounded in her ears.

"Who is it?" The same strident voice of the morning called from inside somewhere.

Arden swallowed and cleared her throat. "Arden Gifford! I want to see DorJo!"

"She's not here!"

"Well, do you know where she is?" Think tough, she told herself. She looked down at her hands. They were shaking ever so slightly.

There was a pause, then quite suddenly a figure loomed in the doorway behind the rusted screen. DorJo's mother was a plump woman with pulled-back hair. Some of the shorter pieces had come out of their pins and were hanging loose around her face. A button was missing from her dress, leaving an embarrassing gap right at her bosom. She rested one hand on the crosspiece of the door, as though she might at any minute thrust it outward and knock a person winding. Arden stepped back.

"What do you want to know for?" Mrs. Huggins asked.

It seemed to Arden that her own mouth muscles weren't working very well. She wanted to bolt and run.

"Well?" Mrs. Huggins prodded impatiently. "I ain't got all day."

Arden opened her mouth and then found she couldn't choose what to say. Because she's my best friend. Because I miss her. Because . . . because.

"DorJo wasn't here when I came by this morning and she never came to school. She never misses school," she managed to say at last. "I . . . we're best friends."

"Oh, really now?" Mrs. Huggins's tone was mocking. "Well, if that's so, you sure ought to know where she is. Why ain't she over at your house?"

The question stung Arden bitterly. "I don't know why," she said in a voice barely above a whisper. "Can you tell me where else you think she might be?"

"Look," said Mrs. Huggins, "I am sick to death of people coming by here trying to find that girl. First it was that nosy principal, now it's you. *I* don't know where she is—she left out of here of her own free will Friday night. I didn't run her off—understand?"

"But DorJo wouldn't just go away for no reason!"

Her own boldness terrified her. Mrs. Huggins's eyes narrowed to little slits. She pushed open the screen and came out on the porch. She was barefooted. Arden mentally gauged the distance from the porch to the ground, in case she had to jump backward and hit the ground running.

"Whatever the reason, it ain't any of your business," Mrs. Huggins said, her voice hard as iron. "What goes on in this house is family business."

"But DorJo's my friend—" Arden felt the trembling of her legs all the way up to her teeth. Maybe they wouldn't even hold her up when she started to walk away.

"Well, that's real sweet!" Mrs. Huggins didn't sound as though she thought it was a bit sweet. "Let me tell you something, young lady—DorJo got herself into this and she can get herself out. Any girl talks to her mother the way she has

59

talked to me don't deserve to be worried about!" Then, as though she realized she had said more than she intended, she turned away abruptly and started back inside, muttering under her breath.

Frightened as she was, Arden felt that she couldn't give up yet. "W . . . would Jessie know where I could find DorJo?"

"I don't know!" the woman shouted. "I am right here by myself. Jessie left Saturday and I don't know where she went. You'd think them two girls would be happy we was all here together, but no—they act like I've got to have their permission to spit around here! Well, it's my house and they'll do what I say or . . . or they can do what they done, which is get out!"

Arden stumbled down the steps, feeling that all her muscles had come undone and were flapping loose like clothes on a line. In her whole life she had never met a grown-up like Mrs. Huggins. She walked for quite some way before she began thinking clearly again. The slosh of the water jar in her backpack reminded her of her mission.

Although they hadn't been there since August, Arden thought that if she were going to run away from home, the hideout would be the first place she'd go. She would never forget the day DorJo led her to the clay bluffs at the north end of Haverlee. There, behind kudzu and honeysuckle, a little cave had eroded under roots of great trees. It wasn't deep enough to be scary, but two people could sit in it comfortably. DorJo had brought pine straw to cover the clay floor and had scraped the walls to make them smoother. Even in cold weather it was pleasant if the sun was shining. The walls served as a windbreak and absorbed the sun's warmth. Last year they had spent hours together there. It was a spaceship, a house, a theater, a school, a plane, a raft. When the kudzu died after the frost, they piled dead branches around so no one would discover the place.

Please be in the hideout, DorJo.

She thought it so hard she could almost hear the words.

She stopped for a moment at the City Limits sign and bent to tie her shoe, looking all around as she did so to see whether anyone was watching her. Two or three men hung around the entrance to Fudge's Store, but they took no notice of her. Shades were drawn at Norman Cheswick's house. Quickly, Arden turned right and went down a row in Mr. Cheswick's cornfield. Most of the ears had long since been pulled, but the stalks remained, brown and drying. Some had fallen and lay in the dirt. Others leaned at precarious angles. An occasional ear, its tassels burned to a crisp by endless days of sunshine, clung to the stalk like a koala baby to its mother. The afternoon breeze stirred the dry leaves, making them wave and whisper as she passed.

It was a long row, curving slightly to the left. By the time she reached the end of it and looked back, she was completely out of sight of the highway.

Now her steps quickened as she went along a narrow dirt road. The dirt wasn't powdery or thick enough to hold footprints. For all she could tell, no one had traveled it in days, but it could just as easily have had someone on it less than an hour ago. At a certain large beech tree, she took one last look around and slipped into the woods. Within a few minutes she had reached the cave.

With the help of some tree roots protruding from the clay, Arden pulled herself up to the cave entrance and looked in.

It was empty.

Not until that instant did she realize how much she had counted on DorJo's being there. The emptiness of the cave was like a physical blow, a disappointment so profound that for a moment she refused to accept it.

She climbed dispiritedly into the cave, turned, and sat facing outward. The straps of the pack bit into her shoulders and she shrugged it off onto the pine-straw floor. The cave was just as they had left it in August, with colored rocks and bits of glass lining a little ledge on one side, and two yellow plastic cups turned down side by side against the back wall. Everything was still except for a horsefly buzzing in and out. She stared glumly through the kudzu curtain that hid the cave from the outside world. It was the first time she'd ever been here alone. She did not like the feeling.

If DorJo were here we'd light into the food, she thought. The Vienna sausages would taste really good.

Restless, she looked about her, examining the cave closely for any sign that her friend might have been here. Perhaps she left a note inscribed upon the clay wall with one of the pointed blades of the Swiss Army knife.

She could find nothing new or different. She untied the pack and pulled out the chips. Munching halfheartedly, she composed a note for DorJo, then remembered she had nothing to write with. The floor and walls were much too hard for an ordinary stick to make an impression, and she didn't have a single scrap of paper.

"Dear DorJo," she spoke aloud the note she would have written. "I am really worried about you. If you find this note, come straight to my house. Love, Arden."

What a comfort it would be for DorJo, to know someone was looking for her. That was when she got the bright idea of leaving something of her own for DorJo to find. Her pockets were empty, so she took off one of her socks and draped it across the two yellow cups.

She opened the jar of water and drank some of it. The rest she left, along with the raisins and the Vienna sausages. She felt a little more useful, then, having done something real for

DorJo. Tying the pack shut once more, she slid down the bluff and started back home.

As Arden entered the house, she heard Mom's quick footsteps overhead and, in a moment, saw her sandaled feet at the top of the stairs. She had changed from her hospital uniform into an oversized T-shirt and soft cotton pants. She looked awfully good to Arden—nothing at all like Mrs. Huggins. Impulsively, Arden reached out and gave her a great hug when she got to the bottom step.

"My stars!" Mom laughed, returning the squeeze. "What a welcome! I believe I'll go back upstairs and come down again. Where've you been?" She helped Arden remove the backpack.

"I've been looking for DorJo," said Arden. "Mom, she's disappeared."

"What? Are you serious?"

"Yes. She's really gone. Her mother hasn't seen her since Friday night. I'm scared." It was the first time she'd said the words aloud, and without warning the backed-up tears spilled down her cheeks. Mom steered her into the living room and they sat on the sofa.

"Tell me," she said.

As best she could, Arden told everything that had happened that day, including the run-in with Mrs. Huggins. "After I left there I went to look in . . . a place we go sometimes," she finished, sniffing and wiping her eyes. "DorJo wasn't there. It's like she's vanished into thin air."

"And her mother doesn't know where she's gone?"

"She says not, but maybe she's not telling the truth. Mom, isn't there any way to make that woman tell us what happened Friday night?"

Mom shook her head. "No. Mrs. Huggins says this is strictly

a family affair. You can understand that. If we had an argument in our family, we wouldn't want the neighbors coming in to give their two cents' worth."

"Yes, but if one of us disappeared after the argument, they might have a good reason!" Arden argued.

"You have a point there," Mom conceded. "Still, I don't know what we can do if Mrs. Huggins is so determined to keep others out of her business."

"I wish she'd never come home!" Arden said with heat. "DorJo and Jessie were doing fine by themselves. She ruins everything!"

"Come home? You mean, she's been away?"

Arden nodded. "Most of the time, for the past three years."

Now Mom looked really worried. Arden regretted reporting Mrs. Huggins's extended absences. Things like that always got adults upset.

"But DorJo and Jessie have everything under control," she added hastily, to give a better impression.

"It doesn't sound like it," Mom said. "Where does Mrs. Huggins go, and why? Who supports the girls?"

Arden didn't know the answers to any of the questions, so she tried to shift the focus of the conversation. "By the way, Mr. Cranston is going to call around dinnertime to let me know what he found out from Jessie. Maybe she and DorJo are together somewhere."

"Well, I'd like to speak with him, too," Mom said. "I had no idea—" She got up and went off to the kitchen, muttering to herself.

Mr. Cranston's call came just before dinner.

"What did you find out?" Arden asked as soon as she knew who it was. "Is DorJo with Jessie? What—"

"Wait a minute, wait a minute," he said. "One thing at a

time. Let me say right off, Arden, I don't have any good news."

"Oh," she said. She sat down suddenly in the chair by the telephone.

"Jessie refused to talk to me," Mr. Cranston said. "The foreman came back to me with the message that she wasn't staying at home anymore and that she didn't know where her sister was, unless she was staying with you."

"But she's *not!*" Arden interrupted. "I hope you told her that."

"Well, I did send word back to her that you hadn't seen DorJo since Friday, but the foreman said Jessie told him there wasn't anything she could do about it, not to bother her anymore."

"That doesn't sound like Jessie," Arden said. "Didn't she even act worried?"

"I don't know," said Mr. Cranston. "All I know is what the foreman reported."

Arden didn't like the dead-end-street feeling she was getting. She didn't want to hear Mr. Cranston say he didn't know what to do next. "Mom wants to talk to you," she said. "I'll get her."

She hovered nearby while Mom and Mr. Cranston talked, not particularly encouraged by the frown on Mom's face. There was mention of the sheriff, of the Social Services Department, of getting a group of people to go out and "beat the bushes." Listening made her more anxious than ever. Perhaps her face showed it, because Mom glanced over at her and said abruptly, "Mr. Cranston, let me talk this over with Tom and get back to you. Perhaps we can come up with a plan."

As soon as she hung up the receiver she came over and put her arm around Arden. "Cheer up, hon," she said. "I'm sure DorJo is all right, wherever she is. We'll find her."

Arden nodded, wanting with all her heart for Mom to be

right. But it was a scary business. She went up to her room and sat on the window seat, looking out at the backyard. The sun rested just above the treetops and then began to sink. Why hadn't DorJo come to her, at least by now? Was it because she was miles and miles from here? Perhaps she had gone to Porterfield and taken a bus to . . . to Miami. DorJo was brave—she might do something like that. The world seemed an enormous place all of a sudden—DorJo could be anywhere in it.

At dinner when she and Mom reported to Dad and Hill, they were sympathetic but not very optimistic.

"I've read about this sort of thing," Hill said, talking with his mouth full in spite of Mom's you-know-better look. "In cities, if you report a person missing, they won't do anything about it right away. They tell you that in nine cases out of ten the missing person went away on purpose. They won't go looking unless they suspect foul play, or unless it's some little kid that's wandered off."

"Well, gosh! A person could die!" Arden was indignant.

"Hill may have overstated the case a bit," Dad said, giving him a hard look. "We're confronted with a peculiar situation where DorJo is concerned. If Mrs. Huggins had reported her missing or a runaway, the sheriff could have an all-points bulletin out for her. Law enforcement can't do very much until someone brings evidence that . . . it's serious enough for them to be involved."

"Could we report her as a runaway?" Arden asked hopefully.

"We don't know that she is," Dad reminded her. "We don't know anything about it, really."

Arden picked at her food glumly. "If . . . when she comes back, could we adopt her?"

Hill rolled his eyes. Mom and Dad looked at each other.

"Why not?" Arden went on. "Hill's going to live with Gran and Big Dad—there'll be an extra room and everything."

"Well, for one thing, DorJo might not want to be adopted," Mom said. "It's a complicated process. And Mrs. Huggins would have to be willing to give up DorJo forever."

"Oh, she wouldn't care," Arden said. "If she did, she'd stay home."

"That's a bit harsh," said Dad. "You don't really know how Mrs. Huggins feels. Besides, most kids prefer their own parents, even the ones who don't treat them well. I think maybe there are ways to help DorJo without taking over, don't you?"

"I just want to find her," Arden mumbled, placing her knife and fork across the plate the way Gran had instructed. Gran was hot on table manners.

Hill and Dad cleared away the dishes and washed up. Arden brought her books down to the dining room table to work, so that she could be near the telephone if Mr. Cranston called back. Ever so often she would glance out the window, watching the sky color change and deepen. At least it wasn't raining. She couldn't stand the thought of DorJo out in the rain.

She heard Dad call upstairs to Mom that he and Hill were going out and would be back around ten. The house got very quiet. She read the same words over and over in her social studies book, not remembering from one paragraph to the next what they said. After a while she went to sit on the back steps.

Night had fallen and the crickets and frogs competed to see which could make the most noise. It was a nice noise, she thought. It could put a person to sleep. She rested her chin on her hands, breathing the cool air. Her eyelids drooped. Images jumbled in her mind and she drowsed.

"Psst!"

Her eyelids fluttered open and her brain scrambled to right itself. She'd forgotten where she was.

"Psst!"

She stared into the darkness, still too drowsy to be frightened.

Then she saw a shape move out of the deeper shadows of the yard and move swiftly toward her. Astonished, she pushed herself up, her mouth open to shout, but before the sound could come out, the shape emerged in the dim square of light cast by the kitchen window.

CHAPTER 7

"DORJO!" ARDEN YELPED.

"Shhhh!" DorJo shushed frantically, fading back into the shadows. "Come here, out of the light."

Arden thought her heart would burst with gladness. "Oh, Dor!" she said, grabbing her friend in a huge hug. "Pinch me so I'll know I'm awake! Where've you been? I've been worried to death—"

"Don't make so much fuss," DorJo said.

"But we've been looking for you all over—"

"Who has?"

"Me. Mr. Cranston. My folks were about to jump in."

"Oh," said DorJo. "Well."

"We didn't know what to do," Arden babbled on. "Your mother wouldn't tell us anything except to mind our own business."

DorJo was silent. She swayed ever so slightly.

"I went to the hideout this afternoon," Arden said. "I brought food and water because I thought sure you'd be there."

"Well, I wasn't," DorJo said tiredly.

"That's when I got *really* worried. I was scared to go back to your mother, she got so mad when I—"

"You got any of the food left you took to the hideout?" DorJo broke in.

"I left it there in case you showed up later, but there's plenty fried chicken from dinner."

"Maybe I could have a little bit of it," said DorJo. "I'm awful hungry." She sat down on the ground, *plop*, like her legs wouldn't hold her up anymore.

Arden knelt beside her, alarmed. "Haven't you had *any*thing to eat since you left home?"

DorJo shook her head. Arden pulled at her arm. "Come on—get up if you can. You've got to have some food in you."

DorJo resisted. "I can't go in there. I don't want Mama to know where I am."

"She won't find out," Arden assured her. "This is the last place she'd look. I was over there twice today, pestering her on your account. She knows I wouldn't have the guts to do that if I knew where you were."

For a long moment DorJo sat where she was, but then, with a great sigh, she struggled to her feet. "O.K. I sure am hungry."

Arden held DorJo's arm as they climbed the back steps and opened the door. The kitchen light made DorJo squint. She swayed again, and Arden hastily shoved a chair under her. "Sit. I'm going to get you some milk first, to give your stomach time to get ready for real food."

DorJo seemed in some kind of daze. She looked as though all her bones and muscles weighed too much. Arden got milk from the refrigerator and poured a glassful.

"Drink it slow, now," she cautioned, setting the glass in front of DorJo. "Just a swallow at a time."

DorJo reached for the glass and put her fingers around it,

but she seemed reluctant to lift it. "I'm shaky," she said. "It feels like I might drop it."

"Wait—I'm going to get Mom," Arden said. "She works at the hospital—"

"I ain't sick!" The old, forceful DorJo tried to take charge again, but she was too weak.

"Mom's no doctor, but she'll know what you can eat and all. Now, don't move!" Arden raced upstairs and knocked on Mom's bedroom door. Hardly waiting for Mom to say "Come in," she opened the door. "Mom—quick, come down. DorJo's in the kitchen and she's starving!"

Mom moved unbelievably fast, out of bed, where she'd been reading, and into robe and slippers. She beat Arden downstairs.

DorJo was sitting in exactly the same position Arden had left her. The glass of milk was untouched.

"Boy, am I glad to see you!" Mom said, rushing to DorJo's side and giving her a quick hug. "We didn't know what to do next."

DorJo didn't say anything. Her eyes were listless.

"Let me hold the glass for you while you take a few sips," Mom said gently. "Here—lean against me and don't worry about spilling it. You need a little nourishment."

"It seems like I didn't eat for so long I've about forgot how," DorJo said in a hoarse whisper.

"Did you have any water?" Mom asked.

"A little. There was a outdoor faucet in a man's yard not far from where I was."

Arden watched as Mom, with one arm around DorJo's shoulders, held the glass to her lips. DorJo took a swallow, then another. In a moment she reached up and held her hand on the glass until the milk was gone.

"That was good," she said.

Arden was full of questions, but she clamped her teeth

tightly to keep from asking them too soon.

"You're going to spend the night here," Mom said, as though it was already decided, "then in the morning—"

"I got to hide," DorJo interrupted. Her voice rose. "If Mama knows I'm here she'll—" She stopped suddenly, lapsing into silence. She looked sad.

"Don't worry," Mom said. "We won't tell anyone you're here unless you say so. We won't make a move without consulting you first."

Mom whisked about the kitchen putting together a soup-and-cracker meal that DorJo could manage. Even the light food had to be eaten slowly, though. By the time she had had enough, all three were exhausted.

"I'll straighten the kitchen," Mom said, glancing at the rooster clock. "It's time for a couple of schoolgirls to be in bed."

"I can't go back to school!" DorJo's anxiety began to rise again.

"Don't worry," Mom soothed. "You don't have to, but you *do* need a good night's rest. Arden, get fresh towels for DorJo. You can put clean sheets on the bed while she takes her bath. She can use my red robe—it's hanging in the hall closet."

"I feel like I'm in a dream," DorJo mumbled as they trudged upstairs. "I think I'm still out in the woods and I'm having a mirage."

Arden smiled at the word. It made her all the more glad to have DorJo back.

She turned on the warm water in the tub and got out the towels and red robe. "Here—by the time you've finished, I'll have your bed made. You can go straight to sleep—I won't talk to you."

"I hope I don't go to sleep in the tub," DorJo said, yawning. "I'd sure hate to drown, after all this."

72

Thirty minutes later they were both settled in the twin beds in Arden's room. Mom had been in to tell them good night and had turned the light out as she left.

"Your mom is nice," DorJo murmured.

"Yes, I think so, too," Arden said. "At least most of the time."

"I bet if you was to run off she'd go after you and bring you back in a minute!"

Arden snorted. "Yes—and she'd tan my backside too. She did that once. When I was four."

She smiled in the dark, remembering that day.

"Mama was glad I left," DorJo said. Arden almost couldn't hear her.

"Aw, DorJo—"

"She told me I needn't to come back."

Arden sat straight up in bed. She stared so hard into the darkness that she fully expected to be able to see DorJo's face. "DorJo, she didn't mean it. Grown-ups get upset and say stuff they're sorry for afterward. She didn't think you'd take her seriously."

"Arden, Mama's not anything like your mom."

There was no use arguing that point. Arden gnawed on one knuckle in the dark, thinking back through the day, trying to remember something that might reassure DorJo. She couldn't think of a single thing. She decided to take another tack.

"Look, DorJo, you and Jessie have been living in that house all along. Jessie's been paying the rent, hasn't she?"

"Yeah. Mama never sent money to help out. One time she went off and owed three months' rent. Mr. Willis let Jessie work it out so we wouldn't have to leave. That's one reason why she had to quit school."

"Well, then, what right does your mother have to run you off? It's not even her house anymore!"

"She's my mama," DorJo said simply. "Whenever she comes back, it's her house."

Arden was hopping mad. She threw back the covers and swung her legs over the side of the bed. "Gosh, DorJo, she's a taker, not a giver! You don't help her by giving in to her all the time."

DorJo was silent. Arden wished that she could see her friend's face, so she'd have a better idea of what she was feeling.

"Jessie left the place Saturday," Arden told DorJo. "Your mother's living there all by herself now."

There was a swift movement from the other bed and Arden was aware, suddenly, of her friend's shape silhouetted against the moonlight coming through the window. DorJo was sitting up. Arden reached over and switched on the lamp between the two beds.

"Jessie wouldn't let Mama run her off," DorJo said.

"Well, you did. How is Jessie any different from you, except she's older? You both ought to stand up to her. Everybody in town would be on your side!"

Arden realized she was ranting. Probably it was the late hour and all the tension of the day. And DorJo's logic eluded her. It seemed to her that all of the right was with DorJo and Jessie.

DorJo shook her head. Her shoulders slumped. "You don't know," she said.

"You're right," Arden agreed. "I don't. But I'd sure like to. I'll try to keep my mouth shut while you tell me everything. I will just listen."

It was hard to believe that the sad, broken creature sitting opposite was her DorJo, toughest hombre in the sixth grade. She thought of the magic moment of Friday when she and Seth and DorJo—full of silliness and contentment—had hauled the two prize buckets of cattails back from the creek.

"Oh," she said, "by the way—the cattails weren't on your

porch where we left them Friday night. Do you know what happened to them?"

To her dismay, DorJo put her face in her hands and sobbed as though her heart would break.

"Well, it started out O.K.," DorJo said, when she was able to talk at last. "Mama had cooked supper, and that was good to come home to. When Jessie works the afternoon shift, I usually have to fix for myself. But Mama was mad I was so late—she was asleep when we left so she didn't know where I was. I should've left a note, but she's been away so much I forget about those things. She . . . she didn't believe me when I told her you and me had been to the creek to get cattails."

"Well, where did she think you were, for gosh sakes?"

The expression on DorJo's face was a painful mixture of shame and desperation. "I don't want to tell what she said to me. They were bad things. She accused me of stuff I . . . I've never even heard of. She talked about me and . . . and boys."

She pounded the pillow beside her with one fist. "If she ever stayed around here she'd know I don't have nothing to do with boys!"

Suddenly Arden was afraid. She resisted the urge to put hands over her ears. She didn't want to hear DorJo, any more than DorJo wanted to tell. "I despise that woman!" Arden burst out, although she had promised herself to say nothing. "I wish she'd go away and never come back!"

DorJo sighed and looked away. "Sometimes I think about it when she's gone, and it seems like it would be so fine if she'd come home to stay. She'd be there when I came home from school, and she'd help me with my homework and all."

"Did she ever do that?" Arden asked.

"I don't know," DorJo said, looking at her in a funny way. "Sometimes I think she did, and then other times I think I made it up. A long time ago I think she was a regular mama."

"What made you run out in the night?" Arden asked, pushing the subject back on track.

DorJo got up from the edge of the bed and began to walk around the room. She didn't seem to know what to do with her hands—one moment she'd stuff them in the pockets of the robe, the next she'd be reaching out, fiddling with something on the dresser or rearranging Arden's stuffed animals on the window seat.

"She went on and on," she said in a low voice, speaking rapidly as though to get it over as quickly as possible. "I finally just couldn't stand it anymore, and I talked back to her. I said, 'If you don't believe me, look out there on the porch and you'll see the two buckets of cattails we brought home!' It was my proof, see, that I hadn't been doing the . . . the bad things she accused me of.

"So she went to the door and looked out and there they were, and she said, 'Get those things off the porch—we'll have cattail fuzz up our noses from now to December!' And I said, 'No, we won't—Arden and I took the ones that wasn't shedding yet, on purpose.' And she said, 'Then I'll do it!' And she slammed out of the door and went over and kicked both the buckets off the porch to the ground."

DorJo swallowed, her eyes wide with the telling. Arden was dumbfounded.

"I . . . I don't remember too much. I ran down the steps and most of the cattails was busted, either the stems or the brown parts. It was so dark I couldn't do much sorting out. I was crying, I was so upset. I couldn't believe she'd be that mean. I stuffed the cattails back in the buckets and shoved them underneath the porch because I didn't want you to walk up and see them like that. I thought I'd go to the creek again on Saturday and get enough to make up for the busted ones.

"Then I went back up the steps and she was sitting at the table, waiting for me. As soon as I walked in, she gave me this look like she'd won over me, and she said, 'I guess next time I tell you to do something you'll do it!'"

DorJo whirled to face Arden, her eyes full of terror.

"I never been so mad, Arden. I . . . I reached in my pocket and pulled out my knife, and I opened the blade and I started toward her. She turned as white as a dead person. She jumped up out of the chair, and she picked it up and put it between me and her, and she said, 'If you come one step closer I'll smash this over your head.'"

Arden could feel the trembling of her own body as she listened to the tale of violence pouring from DorJo's mouth.

"She said, 'You get out of here, and don't you ever come back!' She said, 'If you do, I will call the Law on you and tell them you threatened to kill me. They will put you in the Morley Detention Home so fast, you won't even know what hit you!'

"And I knew she would do it, too."

"DorJo, why didn't you come here that night?" Arden whispered.

"That was the very next thing she said," DorJo answered, sinking down on the bed again. "She said, 'And you needn't to go runnin' off to that little girl's house either. If I find out you're over there, I'll get the Law on her whole family!'"

"But she couldn't do that!" Arden said. "She can't tell us what to do—it's a free country!"

"Maybe not, but I sure wasn't going to take a chance on getting you in trouble, too."

Arden got up and moved over to the other bed. She sat down next to DorJo and put an arm around her. "Look, Dor, we just went through all that stuff on Friday. Best friends look out for each other. I wish you had come over here. It must've been scary, hiding in the woods three days and nights."

"What I did really scared me," DorJo said in a low voice. "I pulled a knife on my own mama. I still can't believe I did it. I didn't cut her, but it seems like I did. It felt like to me I didn't belong anywhere after that."

They sat together in silence for what seemed to Arden a very long time. The electric clock on the bedside table hummed steadily. The hands pointed to 10:30. She felt her eyelids growing heavier, until not even the events of the past day could keep her awake.

"We've got to sleep, DorJo," she mumbled, stumbling over to her own bed. She remembered to snap off the light before falling in a heap among the rumpled covers.

CHAPTER 8

SHE WOKE SLOWLY, FEELING A HAND ON HER ARM.

"Arden." It was Mom, but Arden couldn't open her eyes yet. "Arden? Are you awake?"

"Hmmph," she said. It was the only sound she could manage.

"DorJo's still sleeping," Mom said near her ear. "But you need to get up and get ready for school."

Her eyes flew open then, as she remembered what had gone on before bedtime. Mom's finger was pressed against her lips and Arden nodded, to let her know she wouldn't make any noise. After Mom left the room, Arden turned over and looked at her friend asleep in the other bed. She lay so still she might have been dead, except for the steady rise and fall of her breathing.

While she gathered her clothes and the other things she would need for school, Arden thought about the day to come. In a little place like Haverlee, secrets were hard to keep. If one other person found out DorJo was here, it would be all over town by sunset. Then what would Mrs. Huggins do? Mom and Dad needed to know about the argument and about Mrs. Huggins's threats. Maybe she *could* send DorJo to the girls' detention home. If the sheriff asked DorJo whether she threatened her mother with a knife, DorJo would tell the truth. What she wouldn't tell was what a sorry mother Mrs. Huggins was.

She slid into her place at the breakfast table, aware of the other three pairs of eyes so full of questions.

" 'Morning," she said, taking a large gulp of orange juice.

"Good morning, Bird," Dad said. "I'm told we have company."

"Yes, sir." She looked around the table at them—Mom leaning forward, Hill with one eyebrow raised, Dad wary, as though he wasn't quite sure he wanted to hear what she might tell them. "It's kind of a long story. I might have to talk while I chew."

"Permission granted," Mom said, "so long as the food stays inside your mouth."

She recounted as best she could exactly what DorJo had told her. Hill's expression changed from curiosity to astonishment. Dad and Mom looked very serious.

"What I want to know," finished Arden, "is whether Mrs. Huggins can do what she said—send DorJo to a detention home or get the Law on us for helping her."

"Harboring a fugitive," Hill muttered.

"She's not a fugitive," Dad said to him. "At least, not from the Law. Mrs. Huggins hasn't pressed charges against her."

"I would guess that DorJo's mother was trying to scare her," Mom said to Arden, "because *she* was scared. The fact is, DorJo and Jessie could bring much more serious charges against *her*—desertion of minor children is not exactly condoned by society."

"Well, you can forget that," Arden said. "DorJo wouldn't say anything bad against her mother, not even if she got sent away. It's like to her, mothers have a right to do anything they see fit. It's crazy!"

A small silence greeted her statement. Then Mom said, "Well, Jessie might have a different view of things. After all, she's the one who has had to take the responsibility Mrs. Huggins dumped. Maybe one of us should to talk to her."

"How'd we get mixed up in this, anyhow?" Hill spoke up. "Man, I'm glad I'm leaving!"

Arden flashed him an indignant look. She was about to say something sharp, but Mom intervened.

"DorJo doesn't have anyone to go to bat for her, Hill," she said. "She's Arden's friend. 'We' are mixed up in it because somebody has to be. *You* can help by keeping your mouth s-h-u-t in school and at work."

"Aw, Mom—I'm no gossip!"

"I know," said Mom. "That was just a reminder."

"It shouldn't be too hard," he said, putting his napkin beside his plate. "Before long I'll be a citizen of Grierson. What happens in Haverlee will be of secondary concern to me— except, of course, what happens to *you* folks," he added hastily.

"Thanks," said Dad dryly. "It's good to know that after seventeen years there is still some family feeling there."

"Aw, cut it out, Dad," Hill said, looking a bit ashamed of himself. For a moment a small wave of sadness washed over them. Arden felt it, and she could see it in the others. She wished she could push against something to slow down the days until Hill left. She wasn't ready for him to go. She didn't know whether she would ever be ready.

"Well, then," Mom said briskly, getting up from the table. "*Tempus fugits*. I'm going to call the lab and tell them not to expect me today—domestic emergency. The rest of you wash your dishes. Arden, I'll take you to school. We have to come up with a plan."

Forty-five minutes later the two of them were in the car driving toward school. DorJo was still sound asleep when they left, but Mom had written a note in large black felt-pen letters and pinned it to Arden's bedspread. Arden herself had added a postscript: DON'T YOU DARE LEAVE! DorJo couldn't miss it if she woke before they got back. Arden hoped she wouldn't be frightened in the house all alone.

"I want to go with you to find Jessie," Arden said. "Can't you get me out of school?"

"It seems to me that if you and DorJo are both absent, people will start asking more questions. It'll look more normal for you to be in class, don't you think?"

"What am I going to do when people start asking me if I know where DorJo is—tell lies?"

Mom gave her a worried look. "It does kind of put you on the spot, doesn't it?"

"Yes'm." She was no good at lies, even little ones. She thought about Seth, who would probably be waiting at the door of Mrs. Baucom's classroom for any news she had. She knew he liked her, but she wasn't sure that was enough to make him keep a secret.

"Well, I'll see what I can do," Mom said. "Let's talk to Mr. Cranston."

As usual, Mr. Cranston was overseeing the unloading of the orange buses, so Mom and Arden sat in the car waiting until he was ready to go back to the office.

"I hate for you not to be in school today," Mom said, glancing at her watch. "It'll ruin your attendance record."

"I don't care," Arden said, looking out of the window. "DorJo's not going to get perfect attendance this year either."

Gradually the school grounds emptied. It reminded Arden of water running down a drain, from a great rush to a trickle, to one or two drops. Now everyone was inside except her and Mom and Mr. Cranston. As he crossed the school yard, Mom hopped out of the car and started after him. Arden got out on the other side, more slowly. She looked longingly at the open windows of Mrs. Baucom's room. She could see the mobiles they'd made last week hanging from the ceiling, turning slightly in the morning breeze. She could even see Mrs. Baucom's soft gray hair just above the window ledge—she must be sitting at the desk now, counting the lunch money.

"Come on, Arden," Mom called. "Mr. Cranston's waiting."

She ran, then, to catch up with them, wondering what they had already talked about while she was daydreaming.

Ms. Keys looked startled when the three of them filed into the office—Mr. Cranston first, then Mom, and Arden bringing up the rear.

"Well, this is a surprise, Joan!" she greeted Mom, standing up and smiling more than she needed to. "What're you doing here so early in the morning?"

"Just a little business with Mr. Cranston," Mom said, smiling back.

"Hello, Arden," Ms. Keys said. The tone of her voice altered considerably. Mom heard it. She gave Arden a quick, questioning look that Ms. Keys missed.

"Hello, Ms. Keys," Arden said, ducking her head. She had a sudden anxious feeling that if she didn't follow close on Mom's heels, Ms. Keys would reach out with a shepherd's crook and prevent her from going into the inner office. She felt much better when the door was closed firmly behind them and they were settled in the chairs in front of Mr. Cranston's desk.

"I think you should know," Mom said, getting straight to the point, "that DorJo is with us."

Mr. Cranston looked greatly relieved. "Terrific! I was about to go to the sheriff today and—"

"Well, under the circumstances, I'll have to ask you to pretend you don't know where she is," Mom interrupted. "I don't have DorJo's permission to tell you what happened Friday night, but she's a pretty scared and confused youngster. She's afraid to go home, and afraid for her mother to know where she is. I'm . . . not sure what sort of legal difficulties Tom and I might be getting into if Mrs. Huggins finds out, so until we know where we stand, I'd appreciate your keeping it a secret."

"I certainly understand. Would it be better if she were in the custody of Social Services?"

"No." Mom was very firm. "She needs to be with us."

"Yes," Arden spoke up. "We might adopt her."

"Now, Arden—" Mom began.

"Well, at least I know she's in good hands," Mr. Cranston said. "I only wish that I could get through to Jessie. She refuses to talk to anyone, though."

"I have an idea about that," Mom said, "and I'd like to take Arden with me. Perhaps you could explain her absence to Mrs. Baucom in a way that won't stir up curiosity?"

"By all means," said Mr. Cranston, He looked at her gratefully. "No problem at all. Mrs. Baucom is concerned about DorJo, too. She'll cooperate, I'm sure."

Mom promised to report to him later in the day, then she and Arden left. Arden could hardly wait until they were out of earshot to ask Mom what her big idea was.

"I haven't got one," Mom said tersely, her head way ahead of her feet as she walked briskly toward the car.

"But you said—"

"I'm going to get one real quick," Mom interrupted. They got into the car, but she didn't switch on the ignition right away. Instead, she stared out the window, a slight frown on her face. It was clear she didn't see what her eyes were looking at. She was miles—or blocks—from this place. Arden kept her mouth shut as long as she could bear it.

"So what do we do now?" she asked in a little explosion of breath.

"We go find Jessie and hope she talks to us. I think this is where you'll come in. Jessie might talk to you because you're DorJo's friend."

Mom started the car engine and backed out of the parking lot. Arden thought about what she had said. "But, Mom, where is she? It's too early in the day for her to be at work."

"We'll have to do some detective work without seeming to be doing it. Let's go to the chicken plant first."

The chicken-processing plant lay on the eastern outskirts of town. It employed a great many people who had once made their living farming the land. Some of them still farmed part-time, but almost every family had at least one person working there to bring in extra income. Arden did not like the looks of the place, a flat cinder-block building that covered an acre of ground, with not a twig or tree in sight. On fair days the sun baked the building and the surrounding grounds. Sometimes, if it rained a great deal, the building appeared to sit in the middle of a great, muddy lake. There were no windows to look out or in, but maybe that was a blessing when you considered what there was to see.

Mom pulled the car into an empty parking space in front of the management office. "Come on," she said. "I'm going to see if I can find out where Jessie is staying. You mustn't look surprised if I tell a fib or two—sometimes you have to act a part to get things done."

The manager's office was air-conditioned to what felt like the freezing point. The platinum-blond secretary wore a sweater which, outside, would have made her skin melt off her bones. Arden shivered slightly and hugged her bare arms while Mom asked to speak to the manager.

"Do you have an appointment, ma'am?" the secretary asked. Arden had never seen her before. She must be from another town.

"No, not exactly," said Mom with her sweetest smile. "But I do hope that Mr . . . er . . . Phillips can see me this morning. It's rather important."

"Just a moment—I'll find out if he can see you." The secretary got up and went through a door with a frosted pane.

"How'd you know his name?" Arden whispered.

"I can read," Mom whispered back, nodding toward the name inscribed on the door. In a moment or two the blond lady came back. "Mr. Phillips will see you now, Mrs. Gifford. Right through that door."

It never took Mom long to be on friendly terms with people. Within minutes she was talking to Mr. Phillips as though she had known him for ages. She explained Arden's presence by saying that her daughter was working on a social studies project in school and had permission from the principal to make this visit. Arden hoped that Mr. Phillips wouldn't ask what the project was.

"I do a good bit of volunteer work in the community," Mom said to him. "Just recently I decided to begin a new project and I thought perhaps I could enlist your cooperation."

Mr. Phillips stiffened a bit. His mouth smiled, but his eyes were wary. Arden thought he looked a little too thin—his neck wasn't big enough to fit his shirt collar.

"I'll certainly be glad to help in any way I can," he said, "but I should tell you right away that all of our philanthropic

86

projects have been planned—we really don't have any more money—"

"Oh, no—it's nothing like that," Mom assured him. The relief on his face was unmistakable. Arden almost laughed out loud. "No. What I have in mind is a program for young people in your . . . ah . . . business who may have—for whatever reason—dropped out of high school before graduation. If I can find enough of them, I think I can persuade the local Board of Education to set up programs for them to continue their studies while they work."

"What would you want us to do?" Mr. Phillips asked.

"Well," said Mom, reaching into her purse and pulling out pad and pen, "there's a young woman who works here—Jessie Huggins is her name—who I understand is . . . was a very good 355 student. She had to drop out of school for economic reasons. If I could talk with her, I believe she might be able to put me in touch with others who would be interested."

"Well, I suppose that would be all right," Mr. Phillips said, stroking his chin. He leaned forward and spoke into the intercom on his desk. "Ms. Valentine, would you step in here a moment, please?"

The blond secretary came in. Arden thought it was interesting that her name was Ms. Valentine. She pondered first names for the woman—Bea My, Woncha Bea My, Ura Sweet, and so on.

"Ms. Valentine, would you look at the personnel roster and see which shift Jessie Huggins works, please?"

"Oh," said Mom, "I wouldn't want to bother her during working hours. If I can just find out where to reach her, that will be fine."

Mr. Phillips nodded, to let Ms. Valentine know he'd be satisfied with that. While the secretary was out, Mom and Mr. Phillips made small talk. Arden began to feel anxious. Suppose the only address they had was the one on Purdue Street? Then they'd be back to square one.

Ms. Valentine came back with a piece of paper. "I have here two addresses. There's no telephone for either place. One address is 30 Purdue Street. The other is 201 Hardy Street, both here in Haverlee."

Mom wrote down the numbers in a very businesslike way. Arden wanted to jump from the chair and run out of the manager's office that very instant, but of course she could not. After Mom thanked Ms. Valentine and Mr. Phillips, they walked sedately out of the cold office into the dry, sunny September air.

"Do not," Mom said through half-closed lips, "leap up in the air and squeal. We must be the picture of decorum until we're out of sight."

Arden giggled. "Mom, there aren't any windows in that building. They couldn't see us if they tried, unless they have X-ray vision."

"Oh!" said Mom, looking back over her shoulder. "You're absolutely right. Well, then, in that case—" And *she* jumped up in the air and squealed! "We've got it, Arden! The Hardy Street address must be where she's staying now." Then she sobered a bit. "Who do we know on Hardy Street?"

Arden thought about it. Hardy Street was scarcely a street at all—it was more of an alley, and a dead end at that, about wide enough for one car, and not paved. It was one of the few areas of Haverlee she had not explored much. People left junk scattered around—old washing machines and rusting cars, rotting lumber and discarded road-smooth tires. The yards were usually bare of grass, and quite a few animals ran loose— skinny dogs and cats, even some chickens. Mostly she kept away from there because of the dogs—they always looked so lean and hungry, and they barked with a ferocity that any wise person would take seriously.

"I'm not sure," she said at last. "I guess if we go there we'll find out. I know most everyone in Haverlee, except I don't know where they all live."

"Is that true?" Mom asked as they got back into the car. "That you know almost everyone in Haverlee?"

Arden looked at her, surprised. "Well, sure. Don't you?"

"No, I'm afraid I don't," Mom said ruefully. "Working in Porterfield has put me out of touch. But I'll have to admit I never did get to know the place that well even before I started back to work. Frankly, when we first came here twelve years ago, I felt as though I'd been dumped at the edge of the universe."

"I love Haverlee," Arden said, watching the scenery they drove past as avidly as if she had never laid eyes on it before. "I love it better than any place in the world."

"Better than any*body*?" Mom asked.

Arden turned from the window and looked at her. "Well, all the anybodies live right here—you and Dad and DorJo and Hill—except he won't be here much longer."

"What about Gran and Big Dad?"

"Well, sure—I love them, too. But I like it better when they come to visit us than when we go to visit them."

Mom was thoughtful. After a moment she asked, "Do you think it's wise to love a place so much? What if something happened and we had to move away?"

Arden was not prepared for the question. It was the same as asking, What if I died? A terrifying thought. Besides, Mom ought to know that she didn't *choose* to love Haverlee, she just did. She couldn't help it.

"Don't say that," Arden said crossly, taking a deep breath.

"O.K., I won't," Mom said soothingly. "Sorry."

They rode in silence, turning left on Arbor Street and left again on Monday Lane. Hardy Street was at the far end of Monday Lane. A sign on the corner said DEAD END.

"I wonder how we're going to know which house is which?" Mom said, peering through her window as the car rolled along in first gear. The dogs came out from under porches and ran along beside them, snuffing and barking. "There aren't any numbers on the mailboxes that I can see. Look for 201."

There was only one house in the next "block," an ancient two-story place that must have been there a hundred years. Situated a good distance away from the other houses, it hadn't a visible speck of paint on it. Beyond it, the forest had reclaimed road, fields, everything. To Arden it appeared that the old house itself would soon succumb to kudzu and morning glory.

"I never saw this place before," she said in wonderment. "DorJo and I never came this far."

Mom did not look particularly anxious to get out of the car, but she was not one to give up easily, especially after going to so much trouble.

"Come on," she said, opening the door on her side. "Let's see what we can find out."

Arden turned and looked through the rear window, to be sure the dogs had gone back where they belonged before she set foot outside the car.

The place was very still. They might have been miles out in the country instead of right in Haverlee. They crossed the open ditch on a single board that had been laid across it for that purpose, crossed the weedy patch of yard, and stepped up onto the porch. There was no screen door, but to Arden's amazement there was a rather elegant old-fashioned doorbell on the door, the kind with a key that turned and jangled. Mom turned it and stepped back. Arden wondered if Mom felt as timid and out of place as she did, then decided that grown-ups don't feel like that.

They heard heavy footsteps and suddenly the door opened. A tall, gaunt man in overalls stood there. His stubbly beard was mostly gray and there were deep lines around his mouth. He looked as though standing up was hard for him. When he saw the two of them, his eyes grew hard.

"Good morning," Mom said. "I'm Joan Gifford and this is my daughter, Arden."

The man gave a jerky little nod, but he didn't smile or offer his name in return.

"I'm very sorry to bother you, but I'm looking for Jessie Huggins and I was told she might be here. Arden, here, is a friend of her sister, DorJo."

The man looked from Mom to Arden and back. His expression did not change.

"Whatcha want 'er for?" he said. His voice was like rusty nails.

"I want her help with a project," Mom said. "It's a plan for students like Jessie who've had to drop out of school to work. I didn't want to bother her during working hours."

"Wait a minute," he said. He shut the door in their faces and they heard his footsteps retreating to some place in the depths of the house. They looked at each other. Arden had a case of the dry-mouths.

"Did you ever see him before?" Mom whispered.

Arden shook her head. "If I had, I'd sure remember," she whispered back.

After what seemed like a long time, when Arden was convinced that the man had no intention of coming back, they heard his footsteps again. This time, when the door opened, he didn't seem quite so scary. "Come on in," he said.

Arden blinked. Somehow she hadn't figured they'd be invited inside. She wasn't sure she wanted to go, but Mom stepped right in and Arden followed. When the door was shut she was very conscious of the tall man standing directly behind her.

"Go in that-air-room on the left," he ordered. "She'll be here in a minute."

They obeyed. The room had painted green linoleum on the floor. Feed-sack curtains hung limply at the two windows, neither set of the same pattern. There was a battered chair with one leg different from the other three, and a horsehair sofa. Mom and Arden both sat on the sofa, which, because of its uncertain springs, seemed to buck and roll beneath them.

Mom glanced at her watch, which made Arden remember to look at her own. She'd forgotten to wind it. The hands were still, like the legs of a bug that has died.

"What time is it?" she whispered, pulling out the watch's stem to set it, glad for something to do.

"Ten thirty," Mom whispered back.

Arden set the watch, winding it slowly. The little purring sound was loud in the still house. Time seemed to have come to a halt there. Maybe inside this house it was still 1934 or something.

Why do you suppose Jessie is here? she wanted to ask, but talking in a normal tone seemed inappropriate. She kept the question to herself. Maybe they'd find out when Jessie got there. *If* she got there.

CHAPTER 9

NEITHER OF THEM HEARD JESSIE'S FOOTSTEPS, SO THEY WERE not prepared for her sudden appearance in the doorway. Other times Arden had seen her, Jessie was always neat and well-groomed, so now she was startled at her appearance. Smaller and finer-boned than DorJo, Jessie's dark eyes had the blurry look of someone who has just awakened. Her hair, black and straight, was very long and had not been combed that morning. She wore a white peasant blouse and a gathered print skirt. Her feet were bare.

Mom got up quickly and took a step forward, holding out her hand. Arden stayed where she was.

"Hello, Jessie," Mom said. "I don't think we've ever met officially. I'm Arden's mother, Joan Gifford."

Jessie took the hand briefly and without enthusiasm. She scarcely looked in Arden's direction when Arden said, "Hi, Jessie."

"How'd you know where I was?" she asked, getting straight to the point.

"Well, it's a long story," Mom began.

"I don't have time to listen to a lot of mess," Jessie said.

Arden could see right away that this wasn't going to be the average small-talk conversation. How long before Jessie would have the man—whoever he was—throw them out?

"I understand," said Mom. "I'll be brief."

"You might as well sit down," Jessie said grudgingly. She sat in the chair with the unmatched leg. Mom resumed her place on the uneven sofa, perching on its edge to show that they didn't intend to stay long.

"I went to the plant," she said.

"You're not the only one. I already told the foreman not to talk to anybody about me."

"Well, I didn't go to the foreman. I went to Mr. Phillips, the plant manager. I told him I needed your help with a project I've planned for the plant employees."

Jessie's eyes narrowed. "That's not why you're here," she said, jerking her head toward Arden. "How come you brought *her* along?"

"It may not be why I'm here," Mom said with sudden crispness, "but it's how I found out where you were, which is what you asked me in the first place."

"Mr. Phillips didn't have a right to tell you where I was."

"That's so," Mom conceded. "But he liked my idea and wanted to cooperate."

"Too bad he didn't know you was just looking for an excuse to find me." Jessie shifted in the chair, crossing her legs impatiently.

"I wasn't just looking for an excuse." Mom's voice was even. "Let's say we wanted to find you for two reasons—the one I just mentioned, and another one. Arden is really the one who needs to talk to you. I'll go outside and wait if you'd feel more comfortable."

"It don't make any difference to me what you do," Jessie replied.

Arden's breath seemed to leave her body. Would Mom really go outside and leave her here in this dark room with Jessie, not to mention the lanky man who lurked somewhere near? What would she say? Her mind was as empty as an abandoned house. Jessie's look of stubborn contempt did not help matters. Then she thought of DorJo, and that gave her courage. After all, until now Jessie had always been friendly toward her.

"Do you know what happened Friday night between your mother and DorJo?" she asked.

"DorJo tried to kill Mama," Jessie said rapidly.

"You don't really believe that, do you?"

"It's what Mama said, and she was there. It don't really make any difference if it's the truth or not, though. What it boils down to is we can't live in the same house together—*I'm* sure not going to. That woman has caused nothing but tribulation for years. I've put up with her mess on DorJo's account, because Dor always thinks the next time Mama comes home she'll be different and sweet and everything will be better." She turned away, folding her arms across her chest. "*I'm* the one should've knifed her," she muttered.

"Is that why you left?" Mom asked quietly.

Jessie was silent.

"You weren't there the night they argued," Arden said, "so maybe you've only heard your mother's side of the story."

Jessie's eyes flickered. "Have you talked to DorJo?"

"Yes."

The air in the small room was tense, as though everyone had forgotten how to breathe.

"Did you think about going to look for DorJo when you found out she'd run away?" Arden asked.

Jessie's eyes flickered again. This time she looked at the

floor, tracked the passage of a fly crawling along the edge of the linoleum. "I figured she'd gone straight to your house. It never crossed my mind that she'd do anything else. I never knew any different till Mr. Cranston came to the plant yesterday. Where *did* she go?"

"Out in the woods. She stayed out there hiding three days and nights." Arden's anger began to rise. "All that time she was scared to death, without any food, thinking the police were after her, and nobody—"

"Look, Miss High and Mighty, don't yell at me!" Jessie pushed herself up from the rickety chair. "I've done everything I know to make up for the bad things Mama has done to us. I quit school and took a job so DorJo and me wouldn't get separated and sent to foster homes. Just about every time it looks like I'm coming up out of the swamp, going to have some peace, going to get ahead, *she* comes back. She finds the money I've hid and spends it. She runs up a whole bunch of debts and then goes off and leaves me to pay them!"

She had begun to cry by that time, a dry crying like the whimpering of an animal caught in a trap.

"I am wore out!" she cried. "I don't know what else to do! I don't know how to convince Dor that there's nothing reliable about Mama anymore, and she needn't to sit around waiting for it to happen!"

"I'm sorry," Arden said miserably. "I didn't mean it like it sounded."

Mom got up and went over to Jessie. She put an arm around her shoulder and hugged her without saying anything. Jessie sniffed loudly and wiped her eyes with the back of her hand.

"Where's DorJo now?" she asked after a few moments.

Mom and Arden exchanged glances. "She's at our house," Mom said. "But she's afraid. She doesn't want anyone to know where she is. She thinks if she comes out of hiding your mother will have her sent to a detention home."

"She's about crazy enough to do it," Jessie muttered, looking out of one of the windows.

"You know, you and DorJo don't have to bow to that kind of threat," Mom went on. "If either or both of you testified to what your mother has done during these past few years, the shoe would be on the other foot."

"What are you talking about?" Jessie asked.

"It's your mother who has done things bad enough to be sent to jail," Mom said. "Abandoning the two of you, taking the money you've earned and squandering it, leaving debts for you to settle—"

"Are you saying for us to send *her* to jail?"

"Not necessarily. But if she realized that your case is stronger than hers, she might change her way of doing things."

Jessie moved away from Mom's encircling arm and walked over to the window. Arden did not know when she had ever seen a person look so sad.

"She *is* my mama," she said at long last. "She has had some hard luck in life and didn't get much help. I don't care what she's done, I ain't going to be the one gets her in trouble."

"Are you going to stay here?" Arden asked.

"Yes—at least till she picks up and leaves again."

"Do you feel safe here?" Mom asked, looking around the room.

"Yes." The answer was firm and final, discouraging any further questions.

"It would mean an awful lot to DorJo to see you and talk to you," Mom said.

"I don't know when it could be," said Jessie. "I go to work at three and don't get off till eleven. She goes to school till three and she's in bed before I get off. I'm asleep when she gets up to go to school."

"She's not in school today," Arden said. "She's afraid your mother would come and yank her out. Maybe if you came with us now, you and DorJo could decide what to do next—"

"I already know what I'm going to do. I'm going to stay here and go to work every day. When I find out Mama's got tired and left again, I'm going back to the house. The rent's being paid, only she don't know that. She'll leave when she thinks she's gone as long as she can without paying it."

"Don't you even want to see DorJo?" said Arden.

Tears made tracks down Jessie's cheeks, but she made no sounds. Her hands made unconscious washing motions, squeezing, moving, rubbing each other. Finally she spoke, her words barely audible.

"Yes, I do. But I'm scared it'll make me go back on my plan. It won't do me one bit of good to see her. She'll want Mama and her and me to all be together again. She'll try and talk me into it. I wish you'd go on and leave me alone!"

Arden looked at Mom, wanting her to take charge and make things work out right. But Mom looked as perplexed as she herself felt.

"All right," Mom said. "I understand how you feel, but if you change your mind, you know where you can find DorJo. We'll take good care of her, but that's no substitute for seeing you. She feels cut off."

"Yes—she feels so bad," Arden broke in. "She's afraid you'll think she is some kind of criminal and that you don't want to have anything to do with her."

"Well, you can tell her I'm not mad at her."

"I don't know if she'll believe me," said Arden. "She might think I'm just trying to make her feel better."

"Then I can't help that. What I said is what I said."

There was a long silence after her words. They kept echoing in Arden's head until they didn't have meaning anymore.

"We'd better go," Mom said. "We'll talk about the project another time. Do you think you'd be interested in earning your high school diploma while you're working?"

"I can't think about that now," was all Jessie said.

Arden and Mom walked through the dark house to the front door. Arden half-expected the door to be locked, but it opened easily and they emerged into the sunlight as from a cave. She took several deep breaths as they crossed the weedy yard and the ditch and got back into the car. Neither of them spoke until Mom turned the car around and they headed toward home.

"Mom, Jessie didn't act like herself. She was always nice to me before."

"It's a shame for a girl her age to have so much responsibility!" Mom said angrily. "I don't wonder she's ready to wash her hands of the whole business."

Arden turned in the seat and studied her mother's stern profile. "Are you really going to do what you told Mr. Phillips and Jessie—the program for dropouts, I mean?"

"You'd better believe it! I've been toying with the idea for a good while, but I hadn't gotten around to doing anything." She made a wry face. "Looks like circumstances decided to give me a push."

"I wonder who that man is?" Arden asked. "Do you suppose he's holding Jessie captive or something?"

Mom smiled. "Don't let your imagination run away with you, Arden. Jessie is a strong, healthy girl. That poor man can hardly put one foot in front of the other. If she didn't want to be there, he couldn't do a thing about it."

Reluctantly, she had to agree that Mom was probably right. But who was he? Her eyes scanned the scenery again, picking out what was familiar and what was strange. A new element had intruded into her kingdom—a hole, perhaps, in the fabric. Through it the magic was draining away.

CHAPTER 10

ARDEN HARDLY WAITED FOR MOM TO STOP THE CAR AND PULL up the brake before she was out of the car and running toward the house.

"The door's locked," Mom called after her.

Somehow Arden had thought that DorJo would be waiting right there on the other side to let them in. Impatiently she waited while Mom took her time finding the right key, inserting it, opening the door.

Inside, the house was quiet and still, like an animal holding its breath in the underbrush. Arden went quickly from the front hall through the living room, the dining room, the kitchen. Everything was just as they had left it that morning.

She took the stairs two at a time and rushed into her room. "DorJo?" she called. The bed was made up. The red robe, neatly folded, lay across the foot. The note was gone.

"DorJo, where are you?" She stood still and listened. She heard only Mom's footsteps on the stairs.

"She's gone!" said Arden, as Mom appeared in the doorway. "We shouldn't have left her alone."

Mom didn't say anything. She went over and opened the closet door.

"Aw, she wouldn't hide in the closet," Arden said. "That's kid stuff!"

"Look," said Mom, "you and I don't have even the beginning of an idea of how afraid DorJo may be that her mother will find out where she is. She *might* hide in a closet."

"But her mother doesn't know she's here—"

"That's not the point. When you're afraid, you're afraid. It's a feeling. Remember when you were scared of thunder? No matter how·many times I told you that a sound couldn't hurt you, you still screamed and shut your eyes tight and put your hands over your ears."

Arden sighed. It was hard to argue with a mother who remembered things so well. "Well, what do we do?"

"We keep calling and looking. She has to be sure that it's just us."

Arden went down the hall to Hill's room, calling DorJo's name all the way. She felt silly opening the door to his closet, but she did it anyhow, remembering what Mom had said. Next she checked the hall closet, while Mom looked in hers and Dad's room.

The bathroom door was closed. Mom knocked, then tried the knob. It wouldn't turn.

"She's in there," she mouthed, pointing.

"DorJo," she called. "Arden and I are back with some news for you." They waited. The silence was heavy and immovable.

"You say something," Mom whispered to Arden.

"I wish you'd hurry and get out of there," Arden said to the door. "I'm about to wet my pants!"

In less time than it takes to say the words, the lock clicked and the bathroom door opened a crack. DorJo peered out at them through the narrow slit.

"Is that the truth," she asked, "or are you just trying to get me to come out?"

"Both," said Arden. "We've been gone the entire morning, and nowhere near a bathroom."

"Who else is with you?"

"It's just Mom and me, I promise."

DorJo came out, then. Her eyes darted all about, checking beyond them to the hall, the doorways, the steps disappearing downward.

"DorJo, I wouldn't lie to you," Arden said.

"I guess not." It came out as a kind of despairing sigh. "Go on to the bathroom, if you have to go so bad."

"I'm going to fix lunch," Mom said. "Would you like to come with me, DorJo?"

"I'll wait for Arden," she said, not moving from her place by the bathroom door.

"All right. I'll call when it's ready." Mom retreated downstairs. When Arden came out of the bathroom a few minutes later, DorJo was sitting on the floor with her back to the wall and her elbows resting on her knees. Arden squatted beside her.

"Have you been in there the whole morning?"

"No, not the *whole* morning."

"Most of it?"

DorJo nodded. "I woke up, because all of a sudden everything was so quiet it was louder than noise. The note on your bed said y'all had gone. I got up and put on my clothes and was working up my nerve to go downstairs and maybe get a biscuit or something."

"Well?" Arden prompted.

DorJo looked embarrassed. "Well, the telephone rang. I felt

like whoever it was must know I was here—it rang and rang and rang. I was counting the times without even knowing it. It rang thirteen times. I felt like they could *see* me not answering, and that pretty soon they'd be over here knocking on the door. So I . . . locked myself in the bathroom."

"You mean you didn't even get any breakfast?"

She shook her head.

"Good grief, DorJo! If you keep this up, pretty soon you'll be so thin you'll be able to go in and out of rooms without opening the doors!"

In her present state, DorJo did not think that was funny. "Why aren't you at school?" she asked, changing the subject abruptly. Arden caught the wistful note in her voice.

"Mom and I had to do something else."

"You won't get perfect attendance," DorJo said, distressed.

Arden shrugged. "So what? You won't either, and if you don't get it, I don't care if I do or not."

"You shouldn't've done that. One of us ought to get it."

"It's too late now. Besides, what's so important about being there every single day, rain or shine, sick or well? Now the pressure is off. From now on we go because we want to."

DorJo smiled and shook her head. "You got a reason for everything, don't you?"

"No. Mostly I want you back at school. I don't even want to be there if *you* aren't."

DorJo looked away. "I might not be able to go back."

"Well, you surely can't hide in the bathroom the rest of your days!" said Arden. Then she added, "Mom and I went looking for Jessie."

DorJo sat straight up. "Did you find her?"

"Girls, lunch is ready!" Mom called. "Come on down while the soup's hot."

"Tell you over lunch," said Arden. "Come on."

DorJo was reluctant to come downstairs until Arden assured her that both the front and back doors were locked and that nobody could pop in except members of the family, who had keys. The three of them sat at the kitchen table over bowls of homemade vegetable soup and hot cinnamon rolls. DorJo was famished. Mom and Arden took turns describing their adventure, including the trip to the plant and the discovery of the Hardy Street address. DorJo listened intently as Mom told about finding the house and about the unfriendly man who came to the door.

"Do you know who that man could be?" Arden asked. "I never saw him before, DorJo. I never even knew that house was there, did you?"

Her friend suddenly became very interested in the soup. "Yeah," she said after a moment, not looking up.

"Is the man a . . . friend of Jessie's?" Mom asked quietly.

"You might say that," DorJo replied.

They waited, Arden bursting with curiosity. She had to remind herself that friends tell each other only what they want to tell.

"It's my granpa," DorJo said suddenly.

Arden's eyes widened. Even Mom stopped eating to stare. "I didn't know you *had* a granpa," Arden said. "Not here in Haverlee, I mean."

DorJo raised her eyes and looked at the two of them. "Mama don't know he lives here, and he don't want her to know. He's been here nearly two years now."

"Is it her father?" Mom asked.

"No—it's my dad's."

Every question seemed to raise another. Arden had the feeling that the universe was expanding with great swiftness into long, dark corridors and faceless walls.

"See, it's like this." DorJo put down the soup spoon. "My

dad was in the Army in Vietnam. When I was hardly born we lived on the base at Fort Bragg. After he was killed we moved here because Mama got a job at the chicken plant through some friend of hers who knew somebody else who worked there. It was kind of strange, really, because Haverlee's a good long way from the base. But it was like she didn't want to be anywhere near anybody she knew. She didn't tell my dad's people where we were going, just up and left without no forwarding address."

"How'd they find out, then?"

"Jessie. When Mama first started this business of going away for a long time, Jessie found the address and wrote to them. It turned out that Grandma had died. That part was sad, because my dad was their only child and then their grand-children disappeared, and Granpa claims she grieved herself to death." DorJo paused and sighed. "Granpa came here. First he tried to get Jessie and me to go back to West Virginia, but we didn't either of us want to leave. We thought Mama might come back. So then he decided to find him a place to live somewhere nearby, so we'd have somebody to depend on. He's hid about as good as a person can be, in this little old town. So far, nobody's put together about the last names being the same. He don't want Mama to know he's here because he thinks she'd take us away again and he wouldn't be able to find us next time. He's too sick. It's something with his lungs— he was a coal miner."

"Heavens to Betsy!" Mom murmured.

"I hope you're not planning to tell anybody this," DorJo said.

"Well, we need to talk about it," Mom said cautiously. "Mr. Cranston was ready to call the sheriff's office this morning to get them to start looking for you. It would mean questioning your mother and probably making her angrier than ever. That wouldn't do you any good, so I told him. He's promised to keep it a secret."

DorJo looked worried. "Are you sure he won't tell? Mama'd be over here in a New York second if she knew you was letting me stay here. She'd say bad things."

"I don't care about that," Mom said reasonably, getting up for more soup. "Sticks and stones may break my bones, and all that stuff. What can she do?"

"I guess she can make me leave," DorJo said softly. "I'm not old enough by law to refuse to go with her." She bowed her head. "She don't really want me around, but she'd get me away from here for jealousy. She'd get the Law on you for hiding me and then she'd have me sent to the detention home."

Arden waited for Mom to say it wasn't so, but she didn't. Instead she looked very thoughtful. Arden began to feel hopeless. How could one selfish, angry woman have so much power over people?

She and DorJo washed the lunch dishes while Mom went to telephone Mr. Cranston about finding Jessie. She promised DorJo not to tell about Granpa Huggins for the time being.

"Jessie said to tell you she's not mad at you," Arden said as she rinsed the bowls. "Matter of fact, she sounded as though she would've done the same thing in your shoes."

"I wish we was together," DorJo said in a low voice. "Did she say she'd come over sometime?"

Arden didn't look at her as she answered. This was the hardest part. "No. She couldn't figure out a time right now. Maybe in a few days."

DorJo seemed to accept that, to Arden's great relief.

"I don't understand why you didn't go to your Granpa's house Friday night, or at least on Saturday," Arden said. "Don't you like him?"

"Sure I like him! He's a nice man. He don't talk much,

but it means something when a person his age leaves the place they've lived all their life and comes down here just to keep a eye on two grandchildren. We're all the kin he's got left. He's been good to us, as far as he's able."

"Then why didn't you go there, like Jessie did?"

DorJo didn't answer right away. She dried the dishes methodically, rubbing and rubbing far beyond what was necessary.

"I wanted to. But I was scared of myself—like if I could pull a knife on my own mama I . . . I didn't need to be around anybody I cared about. The awful thing is, I'd already pulled that knife out once before, with Seth and Albert Twiggs. It was just a joke then, but—it was like something way down in me was always thinking about what I could do with that knife. Like I didn't have any control over myself. I was looking at myself and thinking I could kill somebody. I never thought about myself like that before."

She chewed her underlip, frowning at the memory. "It just seemed like I belonged out there in the woods."

"You're too hard on yourself," Arden said. "People have a right to get mad if they're mistreated."

"Yeah—but it's what you do when you get mad that's the problem. See, for that little bit of time Friday night I felt strong and powerful. I felt like a giant." She turned to Arden. "You know I've always been bigger than most of the other kids at school. Thing is, I'm bigger than some grown people, too."

"Well," said Arden, "you could get rid of the knife, or let someone you trust keep it for you."

"I already buried it," DorJo said. "It didn't seem right to throw it away after all the money Jessie spent on it. So I buried it."

"Do you know where it is?"

"Yeah. I could go right to it. But I'm not going to."

Just then Mom came into the kitchen. "I've talked to Mr. Cranston, DorJo. I asked him to help us figure out a way to get you back in school without making things worse between you and your mother."

"Well?" said Arden.

"He had a pretty good idea," Mom said, flopping down in a kitchen chair. "It's so simple I don't know why we didn't think of it."

DorJo put down the dish towel and came over to Mom. Hope burned in her eyes. "How?"

"Well, the fact is, your mother isn't looking for you. She isn't trying to get other people to look for you, maybe because she's not anxious for people to find out why you ran away. Mr. Cranston thinks we can take advantage of that. You simply stay here with us and go to school every day. You'll probably be perfectly safe as long as we figure out how to get you to and from school so she won't see you on the streets."

"But what if some of the kids at school say something to Mama?" DorJo said.

"That's not too likely, is it? First of all, I doubt if they know who she is, and second, I doubt if she knows any of *them* other than Arden."

As Mom talked, Arden thought about Seth. He alone knew that DorJo had disappeared, and thanks to their conversation with Mr. Cranston the afternoon before, he had some notion why. She wondered if, today at school, he had kept his mouth shut when people asked about DorJo. She feared that her own absence might have made him less inclined to keep quiet. Somehow, though, it didn't seem to be a good idea to say any of those things right now. Getting DorJo back to school was more important.

"That makes pretty good sense to me," she said. "Don't you think so, Dor?"

DorJo seemed caught between hope and desolation. She could not seem to frame the words to explain.

"What's the matter, dear?" Mom asked. "What have we left out?"

"I've got no clothes but these. Everything else I own is at the house. I don't know how to get 'em without Mama finding out, and I can't go to school in the same clothes everyday. People would notice after a while."

"Oh, *that's* no problem," Mom said, jumping up. "We have the rest of the afternoon. We'll just go to Porterfield for a new wardrobe."

"But—" DorJo started to protest.

"No buts," Mom said firmly. Her eyes gleamed. "You two be ready in fifteen minutes."

"Your mom is something else," DorJo said, shaking her head after Mom had left the kitchen. "It must be because of her knowing karate. She ain't scared of a thing, is she?"

"Well, sometimes," Arden said truthfully. "But you can hardly ever tell it."

CHAPTER 11

WHEN ARDEN AWOKE ON WEDNESDAY MORNING IT WAS POURING rain, a cool September rain that brought smells of autumn through the open bedroom window. She lay still for a few minutes in the dawn-gray room, listening to the sound and feeling inexplainably sad.

Why should she feel sad? There was DorJo sound asleep in the other bed, just like a regular sister. The shopping expedition had produced a dress, a plaid skirt, a blouse, a sweater, new jeans, a shirt, underwear, shoes, socks, comb, brush, and toothbrush. They had had terrific fun last night dividing the closet into two spaces and emptying bureau drawers to make room for the new things. Really, it was better than having a sister, because she and DorJo got along better than real sisters.

The blue feeling persisted as she went down the hall to the bathroom. She ran cold water into her cupped hands and sloshed her face to get her eyes open. Then she brushed her teeth, staring into the medicine cabinet mirror without really looking at herself. Instead, she was seeing DorJo again at Kilby's Department Store, regarding herself in the long triple mirrors as though she could hardly believe she was the person in the new clothes.

Mom had been the most excited of all. She kept pulling things from the racks for DorJo to try on until finally DorJo stomped her foot and said, "No more!"

Mom blinked in surprise.

"I'm sorry," DorJo mumbled, her hands hanging beside her as though she didn't know what to do with them. "I appreciate you buying me some school clothes, Miz Gifford, but this is too many. They cost too much."

"But DorJo, it's my pleasure!"

"I don't see how," said DorJo. "That's a lot of money to spend on somebody that's not even kin to you."

"Someday you'll understand," said Mom.

"I'm gonna pay you back," DorJo said stubbornly.

"Just do the same thing for someone else when you're able," Mom said. "For now, let's forget it—the paying back part, I mean."

Arden wondered if DorJo could forget it—she was terribly proud.

There was a knock at the bathroom door. "Aardvark? Is that you in there?"

She opened the door for Hill, who stood there in his underwear. His hair was tousled and sleep wrinkles crisscrossed his face and chest. All of a sudden she knew why she was sad.

"Yes, it's me all right, and you'd better be glad of it!" she scolded. "What if it was DorJo and she saw you in your practically nothings?"

"It wouldn't bother *me*," he said in a voice still fuzzy with sleep.

"Well, it would *her*," Arden retorted. "You ought to have a little consideration. She's not used to brothers."

112

"More's the pity," he said, grinning at her. "Are you through in here, or should I set up my pup tent in the hall and wait?"

"I'm through." She tried to look stern, but found it impossible when she thought of Hill patiently setting up a tent in the hall, complete with a small campfire. Gosh, she was going to miss him!

DorJo was just beginning to stir when Arden got back to the room. "Is it already morning?" she groaned. "I feel like I only went to sleep fifteen minutes ago."

"That's what we get for talking so late last night," said Arden. "But I'm not sorry."

"No." DorJo rolled over and eased out of bed. She went to the window and looked out at the rain. "I'm sure glad I'm not sleeping out in that."

"I'll say! Rain's fine when you've got a roof over your head."

DorJo was silent for a moment, watching the rain. "I can't stay here long," she said. "It's not right for me to be living off of your folks."

"But you're not—"

"I don't know what else you'd call it," DorJo broke in. "The money your mom spent on me, it ought to've been spent on clothes for you."

"But I don't need any clothes!"

"Whatever. Her buying stuff for me takes away from you and your brother."

"Well, you don't have to do anything about it right this minute," Arden said. "Come on, now—get dressed. We're going to school."

DorJo turned from the window. "Do you really think it's safe?"

"Look, Mom's taking us on her way to work. You can lie down out of sight in the back seat if it makes you feel any better, but I'll bet you a nickel your mother isn't even awake when we go to school. Please don't worry!"

When, an hour later, the two of them climbed into the front seat of the car beside Mom, Arden was near exhaustion from her efforts at reassuring DorJo. The latest crisis arose when her friend realized that her schoolbooks and papers were still at the other house.

"Mrs. Baucom will purely kill me!" she wailed, slapping her forehead. "My math book and my language arts. What am I gonna tell her—that I can't get books out of my own house? And I didn't have a chance to do any homework—"

"Don't worry about Mrs. Baucom," Arden said. "She won't ask a lot of nosy questions."

"I'll write her a note," Mom said. "I'll say that, due to circumstances beyond your control, you don't have access to your textbooks just now."

"Due to circumstances beyond my control." DorJo tried the important-sounding words. She looked at Mom admiringly. "I guess she certainly ought to believe *that*."

Mom was careful to drive to school the long way, to spare DorJo further worry. She pulled up to the covered walkway where students unload on rainy days and hastily scribbled a note for DorJo to give to Mrs. Baucom. "You girls be careful, now, going home this afternoon," she said as they got out of the car. "Go by the way I told you—no side trips, understand?"

"Yes'm." Arden waved until Mom was on her way up the street, then she and DorJo turned to go inside. She had never seen DorJo so nervous at school. Usually she paraded through the place like it belonged to her and she was just letting all the other people use it. Today, though, she did not want to be noticed. She appeared to be trying to make herself smaller. She hunched her shoulders and kept her eyes downcast—even walking a fraction of a step behind Arden. Just as they were

114

passing Mr. Cranston's office, he stepped out into the hall.

"Well, DorJo—so glad to see you this morning!" His face showed how glad he really was, but for a couple of seconds Arden feared her friend might faint right on the spot. DorJo's eyes darted about like she was looking for a hole to dive into.

Right away Mr. Cranston seemed to know how she felt. "It's good to have you back," he said, lowering his voice. With all the noise in the hall, no one took any notice of them anyway. "Let me know if you need me for anything."

DorJo smiled weakly. "Yessir. Thanks."

He waved them on and went back to his morning duties.

"For pete's sake, DorJo, it's all right!" Arden whispered. "Don't be so nervous."

"I'm not nervous—I just don't want people paying me any attention!"

Unfortunately, as they rounded the corner to the fifth- and sixth-grade classrooms, they came face to face with Nina Wall.

"Gollee, DorJo! Where've you been? Aren't those new jeans you got on? They look really good!"

"Aw, phooey," DorJo said. Nina turned around and fell into step with them.

"I don't know if I ever saw you in brand-new clothes before," she said.

"Nina, you don't have to be so tactless!" Arden fussed.

"I was just telling her she looked good," Nina defended herself. "Boy! Things are a mess when you can't even say something nice about somebody without getting jumped on!" She flounced ahead of them into the classroom.

"Sorry," Arden mumbled. "Maybe I overdid it."

"Shoot!" said DorJo. "If you hadn't said it, I would've."

They went straight to their desks at the front of the room, not even glancing around to see who else was there. Mrs.

Baucom looked up and smiled. "Well, DorJo—how nice to have you back!"

Oh, please don't ask why, Anden prayed.

"Here's a note," DorJo said quickly, thrusting it toward Mrs. Baucom.

While the teacher read the note, Arden held her breath. The note about the books didn't ask for DorJo's absence or hers to be excused. Neither of them had thought about that.

"Fine," Mrs. Baucom said, nodding. She acted like it was the most usual thing in the world for a person to be gone for two days, come back dressed in new clothes, and confess to having no books. Last year's teacher, Ms. Nicholson, would've had a hissy fit.

DorJo took a deep, audible breath and sank into her seat. For the first time she looked as though she believed things might turn out O.K. after all.

Arden leaned toward Mrs. Baucom and whispered, "Did Mr. Cranston explain to you about me being out yesterday?"

"Yes," she whispered back. "It won't be counted as an absence on your record if you make up the work."

Arden tried not to appear too astonished. She wondered what Mr. Cranston had told Mrs. Baucom. Whatever it was, now she was back in the running for a perfect attendance prize.

The bell rang just then and Mrs. Baucom stood to call the class to order. This time she didn't ask the students for information about the people who were absent. Arden was impressed with the way she didn't do anything to call attention to the fact that she and DorJo were back. When the class finally settled down to work, Arden sneaked a glance around the room. Seth was looking at her. She had the feeling he had been looking at her for quite some time and had just been waiting for her to acknowledge his presence. She gave him a quick nod and turned back to her open social studies book.

Although she stared and stared at the words on the pages before her, nothing would stick in her mind.

For sure she didn't want Seth to be an enemy again, but how much could he be told? In spite of the good ending to Friday's adventure, Arden was pretty sure that DorJo would treat Seth much as she always had. Now she realized her mistake in not telling DorJo about Seth's interest in helping find her Monday. She rubbed her forehead hard, trying to think what to do.

"Do you have a headache, Arden?" Mrs. Baucom inquired softly.

Arden looked up quickly. "Oh, no, ma'am! I was . . . just trying to think."

"I wasn't sure, with you rubbing your head like that."

Arden felt her face grow hot. "I'm fine," she said, putting both hands in her lap out of sight.

After social studies and math, Mrs. Baucom gave a fifteen-minute break. Out came snacks from home. Students were allowed to talk quietly to each other, to go to the bathroom or to get water, or to work on projects. DorJo and Arden sorted out bulletin board pictures for Mrs. Baucom at the back of the classroom, munching on apples Mom had given them that morning.

Seth sauntered over, smiling but cautious. "Hey!" he said to DorJo. "Welcome back."

"Thanks." She wouldn't look at him. "What do you think of this one, Arden?" She held up a picture of a pumpkin. Seth might as well have been a piece of furniture.

"It's O.K.," Arden said. "Put it in the stack. Have a seat, Seth. We're looking for fall pictures. You can help if you want to."

"Says who?" DorJo asked, sitting up straighter. "How many people do we need for this job, anyhow?"

"Oh, come on, DorJo. There must be a hundred pictures to sort through. Just hand Seth a bunch of them. We'll get through quicker." Arden tried to sound cheerful. DorJo's eyes turned hard. She took an extra large bite out of her apple and threw the rest into the nearest wastebasket.

"Y'all go ahead and finish," she said. "I've got something else I need to do." She got up and went back to her desk. Arden watched her go, wondering how she had gotten caught in this between place.

"What's the matter?" Seth asked. He sat in the chair DorJo had vacated.

"Nothing," she said hastily. "Everything's fine—really." It was very awkward—she didn't want to hurt Seth's feelings because he didn't deserve it, but she didn't want DorJo mad at her. "Here—look through these pictures. We don't have much more time."

"People was asking yesterday," he said, sifting through the pictures halfheartedly. "They was wondering what was going on—you two don't miss school if you can help it."

"What did you tell them?"

"Nothing." He looked at her, bewildered. "Why would I tell 'em anything?"

"Thanks," she said, more relieved than she had thought possible. "As it turns out—well, I guess I got too carried away Monday." She worked at sounding nonchalant. "With my imagination I ought to be a mystery writer!"

Seth merely looked at her, his steady eyes waiting for her to become her real self again. She felt trapped.

"Thanks for sticking by us, even if I did kind of blow up the situation," she went on, emphasizing the "us." "This'll probably teach you not to take me too seriously when I get all excited about something."

"Well," he said after a moment. "I'm glad it turned out all right."

Mrs. Baucom rang the little bell on her desk, the signal that break was over. Arden went back to her seat. DorJo was reading a book and wouldn't look up.

"Dor, I have to talk to you," Arden whispered as she opened her language arts book.

"What about?"

"About Monday—"

"Girls, no more whispering now. It's time for language arts."

Arden didn't know when she had ever had the fidgets so bad. She thought that she would pop wide open if she and DorJo didn't settle the trouble between them soon.

Even during lunch period it was hard to find a place to talk. Arden made a stab at it while they waited in line in the cafeteria, using the noise as a cover while she tried to explain to DorJo.

"I think you ought to know," she said, "that Seth was with me when I talked to Mr. Cranston on Monday afternoon. He knows that you and your mother had some kind of an argument because Mr. Cranston said it in front of him."

She was not prepared for the scowl that darkened DorJo's face. "Why was *he* with you? It wasn't none of his business!"

"Well, after the three of us had such a good time Friday evening, he wanted to help out," said Arden. "He volunteered."

"After *who* had such a good time Friday evening? I hope you've not forgot what trouble that little bugger caused us, him and Albert. The only reason he got so tame was because I had my knife!"

"DorJo, I was scared Monday. I didn't know what had happened to you. It seemed good to have somebody else around that cared, too."

DorJo shook her head in disgust. "You can't make me believe Seth Fox gives two hoots whether I live or die. You're the one he cares about."

"He's a nice person when you get to know him—"

"So when did you get to know him—while I was gone?" DorJo's voice got louder. Arden shushed her, fearful that she'd be heard even above the cafeteria noise.

"No. I hardly talked to him at all. That's the truth."

"Why didn't you tell me this before?" DorJo asked.

Arden had already been asking herself the same question. "Because I thought you'd be mad," she said miserably.

"Well, you were sure right about that!" DorJo turned away. "You just wait—he'll be spreading tales all over Haverlee about me and Mama."

"No, he won't. I told him at break that everything was fine— that I'd gotten carried away with my own imagination and had blown it up all out of proportion." She felt that she was babbling, but she was desperate to convince DorJo of her loyalty.

DorJo turned back to her. "Out of proportion, huh?" She made the p's puff like the tufts of cattail seeds. "You think he believed you?"

"Of course." She said it with more confidence than she really felt. She remembered Seth's steady gaze. "Dor, I think it would be a mistake to be mean to him."

"Are you peaching to me?"

Arden felt like crying. The sadness of early morning came back in a rush, threatening to overwhelm her. Blinking back tears, she shook her head, mad at herself for being a crybaby, mad at DorJo for acting so stubborn and unreasonable.

"Just forget it," she said. "We won't talk about it anymore."

When they walked down the side steps at the end of the

school day, the rain had stopped, but clouds hung like soggy cotton over the town. Arden felt like those clouds looked— heavy and dark, and ready to weep at the slightest provocation. She thought about the warm glow of last night when they had been as close as sisters. Now it seemed they had lost ground, were back to where they'd been last year when they first got to know each other . . . not quite trustful.

"Hey, Arden!"

She looked back to see Seth hurrying after them. Her heart sank. His timing was awful! She stopped to wait for him, but DorJo kept on walking.

By the time he caught up, panting a bit from his exertions, DorJo was yards ahead. Arden walked fast to close the gap between them.

"Y'all going home?" Seth asked, falling into step beside her.

"Sure." She had to remember that Seth didn't know "home" for DorJo was now the Giffords' house.

"Well, why are you going *this* way?" he asked. "It's the long way around."

"We . . . have an errand to run first," she said. Telling an out-and-out fib made her feel terrible. Up ahead, DorJo's pace slowed somewhat. When they finally caught up with her, she kept her eyes straight ahead, pretending that Seth wasn't even there.

"Where are y'all heading?" he asked. "On this errand, I mean?"

DorJo flashed Arden a look that said, You got us into this, now get us out.

"To Delway's Grocery," Arden said, snatching the first idea that presented itself. "I . . . have to get a going-away present for my brother. He's moving to Grierson in a week or so."

"I'll walk that far with you," he said.

Oh, help, she thought. There were two quarters in the

pocket of her jeans. What could she buy for fifty cents, including tax, that would be convincing?

"You two wait out here for me," she said. "It should only take a couple of minutes."

"I might go in, too," Seth said.

"No!" Arden came close to shouting. "Look—just don't follow me so close. It makes me nervous."

A flicker of amusement showed in DorJo's eyes. "I'm going to sit here under this tree," she said, moving away from them.

Arden turned and went into the store. Delway's Grocery was small and cramped. The aisles jammed up on each other coming and going. A person knew better than to go tearing around the ends because you could come upon some little old lady carrying a carton of eggs and have a messy accident.

Up and down the narrow aisles she went, looking at prices and fingering the two quarters. Thirty-five cents was a good safe price—no more than that. Maybe for that amount she could find a decent candy bar for Hill. She rounded the end of one aisle and started up the next one. Smack in front of her, not eight feet away, was DorJo's mother, studying labels on some cans of fruit. Arden's heart dropped away. She was frozen to the spot.

But in the next instant her brains and muscles began to work again. Turning swiftly, she ducked out of sight before Mrs. Huggins saw her. Without pausing she headed for the Out door.

"Did you find what you wanted?" the checker asked. She was sitting on the counter by the cash register waiting for someone to buy something.

"No—I didn't bring enough money," Arden said, moving past her to the door. "I'll be back."

Arden ran to the tree. "Come on, Dor—now! We got to go. Quick!"

"What did you buy?" Seth asked, coming over.

"What's the hurry?" DorJo asked.

"Your mama's in there!" Arden whispered. "Come *on!*"

Her words had the effect of a lightning bolt. Without a word, DorJo rose to her feet and struck out running. Arden ran after her, the book pack bouncing heavily against her back. She didn't even think of Seth again until, just at her elbow, she heard him say, "Did you shoplift something?"

"*No*, you ninny!" She was shocked that he'd even think such a thing. "Can't tell you now!" She pounded on, DorJo still way in front. "Take a right, Dor, on Green's Alley!"

Not until they had turned the corner did they dare slow down to catch their breath. Seth was still with them, like a determined horsefly.

"Are you girls in trouble or something?" he asked, gasping. "What's . . . going on?"

"Seth Fox, did it ever occur to you that maybe none of this is any of your business?" DorJo stormed, breaking her silence toward him. "I never saw anybody like you that'd just keep hanging around whether he was wanted or not! Can't you find somebody else to pester, for pete's sake?"

Her outburst took him completely by surprise. He didn't yell back at her. Instead, something about him just seemed to withdraw, leaving no expression on his face. Without saying a word, he turned and walked away from them.

"DorJo, that was mean!" Distressed, Arden watched him trudging off under the weight of the ever-present book bag.

"Well, I just can't stand him anymore! He's like a little baby, tagging along, asking a lot of dumb questions. Why does he hang around us instead of the boys? I'll tell you why—they won't have nothing to do with him either!"

"DorJo, that's not fair." She made up her mind even as she spoke. "Here—take this key. It unlocks the back door to our house. You go home. I'm going after Seth to apologize."

He was pretty far away by this time. She started after him, half-walking, half-running. She didn't look back.

"Seth!" she called. "Wait!"

He kept walking. She would've done the same if she had been in his shoes. The book pack seemed very heavy now, holding her back like some giant hand plucking at her from behind. She continued to call his name even though he wouldn't look. She knew he heard. The distance between them lengthened, and with it the frustration of the entire day. Nothing—absolutely nothing—had turned out right.

"S-e-e-e-th!" In the cry was all the power of her lungs and vocal cords. As the sound died, her throat, inside and out, felt burned. Seth stopped and turned around.

"Wait a minute!" she called, breaking into a run again, using her last energies to catch up with him. They met in the middle of the street.

"I . . . am . . . sorry!" she said, gulping air.

"What for?" His voice was flat. He looked past her, his pale eyes still expressionless. She heard footsteps coming up behind her and turned just as DorJo caught up with them.

"You're supposed to be home by now," Arden scolded her. "What if—"

"I'm not used to letting other people clean up the messes I've made!" DorJo glared at Seth, but it was hard to tell what the look meant. "I'm sorry for what I said back there."

Seth looked down at the ground. The little muscles in his jaw moved, but he didn't open his mouth.

DorJo kept talking. "I let my tongue loose without thinking about what it was going to say. I really am sorry."

"I got to go home now," Seth mumbled, his eyes still downcast.

"I'm sorry and DorJo's sorry," Arden said. "Please say you forgive us."

"Yeah," said DorJo. "There's stuff I can't tell you, but that's no reason for me to yell at you—it's not your fault."

Gradually his face seemed to right itself, to lighten. At last he looked up, meeting their eyes.

"All right." A hint of a smile played at the corners of his mouth, although it seemed fearful of coming all the way out. He ducked his head. "I'll see you tomorrow."

They watched him go. Once he looked over his shoulder, lifting one hand when he saw they were watching. His step had more spring in it, Arden thought, as she returned the wave.

"I guess we can go now." Her legs felt trembly and her skin damp. She took deep breaths as she and DorJo walked back toward Green's Alley.

Suddenly DorJo stopped. "Arden, I have got to talk. I've been so mean today, I'm about to be sick thinking about it."

"Right here? Can't it wait till we get home?"

"Nope. Here."

It did feel good to sit down. Arden lowered herself to the curb beside DorJo. She slipped the book pack from her shoulders and felt fifty pounds lighter.

"O.K.—I'm listening."

"I blowed this thing up out of proportion," DorJo said seriously, borrowing Arden's words. "I was mad when I found out Seth knew Mama and me had a . . . argument. I felt like you had let me down, buddying up to a boy neither one of us would give the time of day to last week this time. I felt like I couldn't trust you if you'd do that behind my back when I'd only been gone one day."

A lump formed in Arden's throat. She picked up a slender

stick and traced meaningless marks in the bare dirt near the curbing. She could feel tears in her eyes, in her nose. She sniffed loudly, trying to keep all that water inside her head, where it belonged.

"It boils down to just plain jealous," DorJo went on, her voice muffled. "I keep forgetting that one reason I like you is because you get along with lots of folks—you don't go around with a chip on your shoulder like I do. If I had good sense, I'd try to make more friends, the same as you do."

DorJo fell silent. Arden was half aware of a lawn mower's blast from the next street over, an irregular hammer beat from a construction job somewhere, and from a nearby oak tree the high, sweet whistle of a white-throated sparrow.

"DorJo, I don't want another *best* friend," she said quietly. "You don't have any reason to be jealous of Seth. He seems like a nice person, for a boy. He seems lonesome, too. It's like you said—nobody has anything to do with him."

DorJo stood up and stretched her arms overhead. "Truth is, I don't naturally hate him like I do Albert Twiggs. I'm not promising you I'm gonna be his friend or anything, but I'll be nice to him until he gives me reason not to."

Arden laughed. For the first time that day she felt bright and clean, like a freshly scrubbed surface. She got up, retrieved her book pack, and started to put it on again. "That's good enough for me," she said.

"Here, give me that," DorJo ordered, taking the book pack. "If we're both gonna be studying out of your books, it's about time I took my share of the load."

CHAPTER 12

NEXT AFTERNOON, WITH NOBODY MAKING A BIG DEAL OF it, the three of them left school together. Seth talked so much that Arden feared DorJo would take back her resolution to be nice to him. His words tumbled over each other, like the grand rush of a waterfall, splashing here and there with abandon.

"I never heard you say that many words in all the time I've known you," said DorJo. "If I was to add them up from first grade to now, they wouldn't equal what you've said in the past five minutes!"

Seth looked sheepish. "Sorry—I guess I got carried away."

So, Arden thought, maybe he didn't have anyone to listen to him run on. She'd been pretty lucky in that respect, what with her family and DorJo. She decided to give Seth a chance to talk more.

"What do you like to do?" she asked. "I mean hobbies and stuff."

"Model cars," he said promptly. "I been putting 'em together since I was in the third grade. I've got just about every kind there is."

"You like any kind of sports?" DorJo's tone challenged him.

"Yep, I like 'em all right. I don't get to play much, though."

Arden assumed it was because of his size. Small as he was, he didn't have a chance competing with other sixth graders.

"I think I'd be good," he went on. He spoke in a matter-of-fact way. "Specially at baseball."

"Why don't you play, then?" DorJo asked, never much for letting people feel sorry for themselves. "It don't matter about size in baseball if you're good at running and base-stealing."

"I'm not supposed to run."

"Well, buddy, you sure tore out across that pasture the other day!" DorJo snorted. "You were on the other side before I could say 'Scat!' What do you mean, not supposed to run?"

The compliment from DorJo, though backhanded, made him glow. His obvious pleasure almost canceled the effect of his next words.

"Because I've got something the matter with my heart."

They looked at him, dumbfounded. Old people have heart trouble, not sixth graders.

"I was real sick when I was little. It done something to my heart." He gave a little half-laugh, as though it was no big deal. "The doctor let me listen to it one time with her stethoscope. It kind of bubbles."

"But can't they do something?" Arden asked.

"There's a operation," he said vaguely. A change came over him. He began to walk faster. "It would cost a lot of money. I'm all right, long as I don't overdo. I don't want no operation."

"I don't blame you," DorJo muttered, regarding him with grudging respect. "I sure wouldn't want anybody cutting on me!"

128

His revelation had a sobering effect on them. Arden wondered if he feared he might die suddenly. She certainly would, if she were in his place. It wasn't the sort of question you could ask a person, though. It also explained some things about him—his quietness, his being on the fringe. To Arden he seemed all at once to be a very brave person. She bet that she and DorJo were the only students in Haverlee School he had ever told.

Perhaps he regretted his frankness. "Don't y'all tell anybody."

"Why?" DorJo was genuinely puzzled. "If folks knew, you wouldn't have to take all the teasing about being too little and all."

"That don't matter," he said. "Just don't tell anybody."

"All right," said Arden. "I don't know who I'd tell anyhow, except DorJo, and she already knows."

"Yeah, same here," said DorJo. "I guess that takes care of that. You're lucky you didn't tell Nina Wall. It'd be in the Chicago, Illanoiz, papers by tomorrow morning!"

They all three fell into a fit of laughing at that.

"Maybe y'all could come to my place this afternoon," he said when they'd calmed down some. "We've got a pond—well, it's not really ours, but the man that owns it lets us use it for fishing. I built a raft—we could pole it."

The girls looked at each other. Seth lived outside the city limits, a place Mrs. Huggins would be unlikely to pass by. It would be so great to be able to play outside and not worry about being seen. . . .

"Terrific idea!" Arden said, speaking for both of them. "You go ahead. We'll be there in about forty-five minutes."

DorJo didn't say anything, but when a pleased Seth took off in the direction of his house, she shook her head. "Who would think he'd get excited over us two coming to see him?"

"I wish he wouldn't walk so fast," Arden said, worried now about his heart.

"I guess he can take care of himself," said DorJo. It was as close as she would come to expressing her admiration for his spunk.

But when they finally got to Seth's, sweaty and out of breath, it was much later than they had promised. That was what came of having to take the long way around every time they went anywhere.

"I sure hope Seth doesn't think we lied about coming over," Arden said anxiously, glancing at her Timex. The little white house appeared to be deserted.

"We don't lie," DorJo said. "He knows that. He better not've gone off, after all the trouble we—"

The front door swung open before she could finish the sentence and Seth stood there, smiling his welcome.

"C'mon in and see my cars," he called. "Then we'll go to the pond."

"Sorry we're late," Arden apologized as they came up on the porch.

"It's okay," he said. They followed him, a bit self-consciously, into the cheery little house. He led them down a narrow hall. At the doorway to his room he stepped aside to make way for them. The first to go in, Arden took one look and temporarily lost her voice. On every possible surface in the small room, and even hanging on strings from the ceiling, were dozens and dozens of model cars—antique, late-model, and everything in between. A calendar and several posters bearing pictures of automobiles filled up the wall space. On a worktable by the window two models sat half-finished. The room was like a museum.

DorJo whistled. After a few seconds she managed to say, "You don't hardly have room to sleep in here, do you?"

"Nope," Seth said modestly, satisfied at their reaction. "I don't need much room for that."

"Gee, Seth—you ought to bring some of these to school." Arden moved to examine the small cars more closely. She was impressed with the careful, neat work. "You could have an exhibit—show some of those braggy boys what's really good!"

"It must've took you forever to do all these," said DorJo. "How old were you when you started—three?"

Seth laughed. "More like eight. If you have to lie around a lot, you better find something to do or you'll go crazy. A nurse at a hospital bought me the first one. She and Dad helped me put it together. I did the rest of 'em myself."

"You must spend *hours* in here," Arden said.

"Yeah. Don't you get tired of being cooped up?" DorJo asked.

"Sometimes," said Seth. His hand moved absently to one of the models on the worktable, but then he took it back quickly. "Well, come on. Let's go to the pond."

They went out into the sunlight, after Seth stopped long enough to take three large brownies from the cookie jar. The grassy backyard sloped gently toward the pond. The still, green-blue surface was disturbed only by water bugs. On the far side was a stand of trees. Near them a clump of cattails and other reeds grew at the water's edge. To the right a short pier jutted out a little way into the pond.

"If you want to we can pick them cattails and take 'em to school tomorrow," Seth said.

A cloud came over DorJo's face. She turned away. "Where's that raft you were talking about?" she asked gruffly.

"Right down there." He pointed. The raft lay half out of water, its ragged mooring rope looped around a stake driven into the ground. It was made of rough pine logs lashed together and then covered with a platform of planks. The logs weren't very big around, but Arden was impressed with Seth's obvious carpentering skills.

"How many people will that thing hold?" asked DorJo, looking at it with some doubt. "Are you sure it won't sink?"

"It'll hold the three of us," Seth said confidently. He picked up the long pole lying nearby, and in a matter of minutes they were all on board, with Seth poling them toward the middle of the pond.

"Hey, this is fun!" DorJo said. "We could be Columbus on the way to discover America!" Then she looked self-conscious, as though she hadn't intended to be quite so enthusiastic.

"Or Blackbeard's crew, maybe," said Arden, "bringing our loot into Bath town."

Seth grinned. "You want to pole?" he asked DorJo.

"Well—sure." She stood up cautiously, placing her feet wide apart. Seth handed her the pole.

"You just push from the opposite direction than the one you want to go," he explained. "If you put the pole down in the same place every time, the raft will go around in circles."

"Aw, I know that!" DorJo scoffed. She took the pole and Seth sat down beside Arden. Arden lay back on the sun-warmed boards and looked up at the clear sky, enjoying the slightly dizzy feeling it gave her. Crickets in the dry grass kept up a steady chirping. Crows called down to them from the tall pines. Water lapped at the raft's sides like small puppies' tongues. She watched DorJo through half-closed eyes, thinking that her friend looked like the old DorJo for the first time in several days, calm and confident and in charge.

In the days that followed, Arden found that she no longer had to mediate between DorJo and Seth. Little by little DorJo became his champion at school, bragging about his model cars and hinting at his courage without coming right out and telling what she knew. Seth, for his part, accepted his new visibility with quiet modesty. He did not assume a larger place in the girls' life and friendship than they were willing to allow. It made for a comfortable arrangement. Beside that, Seth's pond was a fine place to spend the sunny afternoons. Partly surrounded by trees, it gave the girls a feeling of security that they didn't have in other areas of Haverlee.

For Arden, having DorJo around helped to ward off the sadness that sometimes washed over her when she let herself think about Hill's departure. Mom had even promised that DorJo could go with them to Grierson the next Saturday when they took Hill to live with Gran and Big Dad. Dad called them the Siamese twins, and commented on their helpfulness with the chores. Absorbed as he was in getting ready to move, Hill didn't bother them much, but he was very generous to both of them as he sorted out items to give away.

But outside, in the open air, there was no freedom. Mom and Dad had consulted a lawyer friend, who told them they were taking a chance by not notifying the Social Services Department about DorJo and Jessie's situation. In spite of that, they decided to leave matters as they stood for the time being. The girls promised not to take any chances. DorJo, aware that she might round a corner and meet her mother face to face, was fidgety on their roundabout treks between home and school. Where they had once roamed every street and neighborhood in Haverlee for hours on end, they were now confined to home and school, except for the visits to Seth's pond.

"I feel like a outlaw in my own town," DorJo said to Arden one afternoon as they sat in the Gifford kitchen having their after-school snack. "It makes me tired!"

"Well, look at it this way," Arden said. "As far as we

can tell, your mama's not looking for you."

"You mean she don't care where I am, don't you?" DorJo said quietly.

"Well, I'm just saying I'm thankful she's not on the rampage or anything," Arden said, regretting her lack of tact. "You're not missing any school, you're not in danger, and it's great having you here."

"Do you realize I haven't laid eyes on Jessie or Granpa . . . or Mama since I came?"

Arden started to reply, but DorJo's words got to her before she said something stupid. In the lengthening silence, she had a glimmer of what it might be like to be separated from all the people you loved most. No good fortune could make up for it. After all, here *she* was all in a stew about her brother leaving, but she did have Mom and Dad still. DorJo didn't even have that.

"I'd really like to see them." DorJo sighed. "Even Mama. Maybe enough time has gone by so she's not as mad as she was at first. Maybe she's calmed down enough so we could talk. Lately I've been thinking the best thing I could do would be to go back home."

Arden felt a pang of anxiety, but she didn't say so. What her friend was saying might be true. Perhaps it was time to think about helping DorJo get back together with at least part of her family.

"We could talk to Mom and Dad about it," she said carefully, "only, maybe it would be a good idea to wait until after Saturday, when they've gotten Hill settled in Grierson. That's only two more days."

DorJo sighed again. "I guess I can wait two more days."

Arden, seeing her long face, had a sudden inspiration. She leaped from her chair. "I'll tell you what—let's go see your Granpa right now!"

DorJo's eyes glowed. "Oh, Arden—that would be so great! Do you think we could?"

"Sure. We'll leave Mom a note. She won't mind—I know she won't."

It was nearly four when they started out for Granpa Huggins's house, munching Granola bars and planning their route so as not to bump into DorJo's mother by accident.

"I wish Jessie would be there," DorJo said, more to herself than to Arden. "She won't be, though. It's her shift."

Arden didn't comment. She remembered what Jessie had said about being afraid DorJo would make her forget her resolve to stay away until Mrs. Huggins left again.

"I miss Jessie a lot," DorJo went on. "We have always been together up till now."

"You'll be together again soon," Arden said.

"I wish we could be a family—Mama and Jessie and me. And Granpa, too." DorJo's face brightened. "The four of us. It'd be—" She stopped, shaking her head. "I have to quit thinking about it. It won't ever be that way."

"Well, even if your Mama doesn't want to be family, what's to keep you and Jessie and your Granpa from it?"

DorJo frowned, straightening her shoulders. "But Mama *does* want to be family . . . when she's here."

"Why does she go away?" Arden had never asked the question point-blank before, but it was a missing puzzle piece, something beyond her understanding.

DorJo didn't answer right away. Then, in a barely audible voice, she said, "Usually it's some man. It's been a different one every time. I don't know why she don't pair up with somebody willing to marry her and stay here with us, but it's like she divides her life in two parts—the part with us in it, and the part with her boyfriends. It's like she can't figure a way to have both."

135

Arden absorbed this piece of information as best she could. After a while she asked, "Does she know how miserable it makes you and Jessie?"

"She is miserable herself. *I* have been like that—so out of sorts that I wanted to make everybody else that way, too."

"You have a lot of patience," Arden said. "You and Jessie both take up for her."

"She has had a hard time," said DorJo. "Jessie says Mama loved my daddy a lot. I don't remember him, but Jessie does. She says they were all lovey-dovey whenever he was at home. She remembers being kind of jealous of him because when he was home Mama paid more attention to him than to Jessie."

"It's awful he had to get killed," Arden murmured.

"It seems like Mama has been mad ever since," DorJo said. "About everything. Jessie and me can't do anything to suit her."

"I'm sorry," said Arden. The words were puny. Some things were so complicated and went broken for so long that after a while they looked to be past fixing.

They had reached Arbor Street by this time and turned to go down it. "There are lots of dogs on Hardy Street," Arden commented, remembering the day she and Mom had driven there.

"I'm not scared of those dogs," said DorJo. "They bark a lot, but none of 'em ever bothered me in all the times I've been to see Granpa."

"Well, I'm going to find a stick," Arden said. "Dogs can tell when you're scared. They can smell it. I'll feel less scared if I've got something to smack them with!"

Sure enough, when they turned off of Monday Lane into Hardy Street a few minutes later, the dogs began their barking and baying. As the girls entered their territory, the dogs came out one by one and followed along behind them. Arden hated their quiet padding paws, their snuffling noses. The crooked stick which she held firmly in her right hand seemed a pitiful defense against all that lean hunger. Nevertheless, DorJo was as unconcerned as if they were walking through a flowerbed. Arden stayed as close to her side as she could without actually bumping into her.

They came at last to the old house at the end of the street. Arden marveled again at how well-hidden it was—a person standing at the entrance to Hardy Street wouldn't even know it was there. To her relief, the dogs had left them by this time and gone back to their posts. She followed DorJo across the ditch plank and up to the porch. DorJo twisted the old-fashioned doorbell and they waited. In a little while they heard slow steps in the hallway, then the door opened inward.

The gaunt man stood there, only this time Arden decided right away he didn't look threatening at all. Maybe it was because now she knew he was DorJo's granpa and that he'd been sick.

"Well, girl!" he exclaimed, and then he reached out his long thin arms and wrapped DorJo in a hug. His lower lip trembled and he patted her back awkwardly. DorJo buried her face in his shoulder, as if she'd be happy to stay there forever.

Arden just stood there wishing she was somewhere else until this part was over. It made a lump in her throat. After what seemed like a long time, DorJo and her granpa took notice of her.

"This is Arden," DorJo said. "I've been staying at her house. Arden, my Granpa Huggins."

"How 'do," the man said formally. "I b'lieve you're the young lady was here to see Jessie with your ma."

"Yes, sir." Arden held out her hand and the man took it in his bony grasp.

"Well, come in," he said. He turned slowly and went down

the dark hall. All of his motion was careful and conserved, as though any sudden movement might throw him off balance and cause him to fall.

"How've you been, Granpa?" DorJo asked as they followed him.

"Pretty good." He did not seem really interested in the question. This time they didn't go into the bare living room, but went all the way to the end of the hall and out onto a porch. Farther down the porch was the kitchen, stuck out here by itself away from the rest of the house. He held the screen door open for them to enter, and then he came in, too.

The table was covered with red-checkered oilcloth. Four chairs not kin to each other by shape or color sat around it. An old-timey cupboard, an electric stove, and a small refrigerator were the room's only other furnishings.

"Have a seat." Granpa motioned them toward the table. He opened the cupboard. "Let me see what I've got here that's good to eat."

"We already had our snack," Arden spoke up, and then somehow knew from the look DorJo gave her that she'd done something unmannerly. "But we could probably eat something else."

The man chuckled deep in his throat, a sound so unlikely that it startled Arden. "I b'lieve I got some Baby Ruths in here. Been savin' 'em for you, girl."

"I guess Jessie told you," DorJo said, getting straight to the point.

"Yep." He brought an unopened package full of candy bars and laid it on the table. "She has been mighty upset."

"Yeah, me, too." DorJo's words were almost too soft to hear. "I'd sure love to see her."

He nodded and pulled out one of the chairs. He eased into it as though to keep from breaking something inside himself.

"You could come over here to stay," he said. "They's plenty of room."

She looked directly at him. "I've been thinking about going back home instead, Granpa."

His face darkened. "What you want to do that for? What'll it get you?"

"It's my home. It's where all my stuff is—and Mama, too. I want Jessie to be there, and you."

The man snorted. He got up, rather more quickly than he should have, and staggered a bit, reaching out for the table's edge to steady himself.

"That'll never be," he said, echoing the very thought DorJo herself had expressed in the walk over here. "You might as well get that notion out of your head. Your ma has caused you and Jessie more grief than two young'uns deserve. She ain't going to be different this time. Jessie's just plumb had it—she's vowed not to set foot in that house long as your ma's there."

"But what if she's here for good this time?" DorJo argued. "Does that still mean Jessie'll never go back, even after Mama's proved she'll stay?"

The man looked over at her, his expression a mixture of pity and anger. "Jessie ain't expecting it to happen, let me tell you."

There was a long, long silence during which Arden hardly dared swallow. Then DorJo folded her arms on the table and buried her face in them. Her shoulders shook. Granpa Huggins came over and put his hand on her back in a kind of helpless gesture.

"I'm sorry, girl," he said gently. "Just as sorry as I can be."

"I don't know what to do, Granpa!" said DorJo's muffled, teary voice.

"Do you like these folks you're staying with?" he asked.

"Well, sure," she raised her head, sniffing. "But . . . I can't live with them right on and on."

"You can so!" Arden said. "We already told you that."

DorJo shook her head. "It's the hiding—the staying out of sight. There's no peace in it. Mama will be so mad when she finds out. She'll feel tricked. She'll think people are talking about her behind her back. I don't blame her. If I'm gonna keep on living in this town, I've got to go back home."

"Eat your candy," Granpa Huggins said. He walked slowly up and down the room, rubbing the bristles on his chin. DorJo began opening the plastic bag. She was not interested in Baby Ruths right that minute. Neither was Arden, but she didn't want to hurt his feelings.

"Tell me, girl, what happened that night you run off? I want to hear your side of it."

DorJo's face went white. She licked her lips and cleared her throat. "I . . . don't want to," she said at last. "I can't."

"It wasn't her fault," Arden spoke up, distressed at DorJo's pain.

"What do you know about it?" Granpa Huggins asked her.

Arden felt caught. "I . . . don't know if DorJo would want me to say," she said guardedly, looking to her friend for a sign.

"You can tell him," DorJo mumbled. She folded her arms across her front and hugged herself as though she were cold. Granpa came back to his chair and sat. Occasionally he would reach out and touch DorJo, to reassure both of them.

Arden started at the beginning, with the quest for cattails, how they had gone by the house for the knife and the buckets and DorJo had forgotten to leave word where they were going. She told the whole story, including Albert's and Seth's prank and the consequences. Arden kept looking at DorJo as she talked, for any sign that she wasn't telling it right. The indignation she felt heated her account of events, but she did not add anything to it that DorJo hadn't told.

"That's what happened," she finished, taking a great breath. "Did I leave something out, Dor?"

DorJo shook her head.

"Why didn't you come over here, babe?" Granpa asked gently.

"I felt crazy," DorJo said, looking down at the table. "Crazy and scared. I thought she'd go straight to the sheriff and have me arrested on sight. I didn't want to get anybody else in trouble."

"Where's the knife at?"

"I buried it."

"Good," he said. "No need to have that temptation about."

There was a stillness in the room after that, almost like they had all gone away and left it empty. Arden noticed the golden light coming in the west window, brightening the dull walls and softening the kitchen's bareness. She knew from the sun's slant that it was getting late. Mom was probably home by now and might begin to worry if they didn't come back soon. Yet she didn't feel she had a right to say anything—this was between DorJo and her granpa.

Finally he cleared his throat, as for a pronouncement. DorJo sat a little straighter.

"Jessie feels all right about you, where you are staying right now," he said. "But if you go back home she's gonna start worrying again. She's scared for you to be there with your ma."

"But why? I can take care of myself—"

"The onliest way you can make it is to take everything she does and says with a bowed head." Granpa's voice was like granite. "It would build up and build up till you lost your temper again."

"I won't," she said, but her voice lacked conviction.

"She'd hold it over you, what you did that night. She'd use it as a threat, whenever you didn't do things to suit her. Living like that'll make it hard for you to do well in school."

"She's bound to be lonesome," DorJo said.

The man nodded. "Probably. It's a pity she has run you girls off. But you can't handle the problem all by yourself. Stay where you are, or come here—but for Jessie's sake, don't go back home."

DorJo pushed back her chair and stood up. She didn't make any promises. "We got to leave now, Granpa. Arden's folks will be worried."

Arden stood up, too. "Mr. Huggins, what if you and Jessie and DorJo went together to talk to their mother? Wouldn't it make a difference?"

"I have give some thought to that," he said seriously. He got to his feet with an effort. "Jessie's against it. She has some notion that Pearl would do somethin' terrible to me. I don't know what it would be. I don't care, for myself, but I don't want to upset Jessie."

Arden blinked. She had never heard DorJo's mother's name mentioned before—Pearl. It sure didn't fit!

He turned his attention back to DorJo. "What I'm telling you, girl, is not to go back to the house unless we come up with some kind of plan. Whatever happens, you and Jessie and me have to be together on this. I'll reason with your sister. It'll take some doing, though—she's stubborn on the subject."

"Oh . . . all right," DorJo conceded, much to Arden's relief. "I'll wait."

He smiled. "It's mighty good to lay eyes on you. I'm glad you came."

"Arden thought it was a good idea," said DorJo hugging him. "I did, too."

"I'm grateful to you," he said to Arden. "I'm sorry if I weren't too friendly the other day—I didn't know what Pearl might be up to, you understand."

"Yes, sir. That's O.K." Arden didn't know anything else to say about it. She certainly didn't blame Granpa Huggins for being careful.

The sun was going down when they left the house. Hardy Street people were coming home from work, giving the dogs something else to occupy their attention.

"I like your Granpa," Arden said. "He is smart and good."

DorJo's smile was proud and satisfied.

CHAPTER 13

AT DINNER MOM AND DAD LISTENED WITH INTEREST WHILE DORJO reported on the visit to Granpa Huggins. She described how happy they were to see each other, and she told about the Baby Ruths, but she left out the part that Arden felt was most important.

"Aren't you going to tell what he said to you before we left?" she prompted.

DorJo's exasperated look made her know she had Quit Preachin' and Gone to Meddlin', as some of Haverlee's old folks would say. There was an awkward silence around the table.

"Well," said Hill after a moment, "what did he say?"

"He said I shouldn't go back home . . . yet," DorJo muttered.

Mom looked a trifle worried. "Were you thinking of going back home?"

DorJo bit her underlip and looked down at her plate. "I had give some thought to it. I can't stay here forever, hiding all

144

the time. I don't feel right about it. Somebody's got to make a move, and it might as well be me."

"But your Granpa thinks differently, is that right?" said Dad.

"Jessie's the one that's really against it," DorJo said. "Granpa's going to try to talk her into at least giving Mama a chance. I promised him I wouldn't go back till I heard from him."

"I think your Granpa is wise," Mom said. "When you do go home, you want things to be better than before, not worse. You need to have a plan. Once Hill is in Grierson, Tom and I can do more to help—"

"Sorry my being here stands in the way," Hill said in a funny tone of voice. When everyone's eyes turned in his direction, he gave a little laugh. "Just joking."

Mom gave him a long look. Then she said, "Maybe this is a good time to announce that tomorrow night, we're all going over to Porterfield to the Taylor House. It's a going-away party for you, Hill."

"The Taylor House!" Hill stared. "We can't afford that!"

"Once in a lifetime we can," Dad said. "After all, I figure the reduction in the amount of groceries we'll have to buy after you're gone will help pay the bill."

"Hot dog!" said Arden, turning to DorJo. "That's the ritziest restaurant around here. We can order steak and—"

"Maybe I could just stay here," DorJo said, giving Mom a pleading look. "Since it's a family party—"

"Now, hush!" Mom said. "You're part of the family, too, and as long as you're here, you'll just have to put up with our silliness."

Mom's backward logic was hard to argue with. It silenced DorJo for the time being, but Arden knew that she was uncomfortable. After dinner when they were upstairs studying, she tried to reassure DorJo.

"It's going to be great at the Taylor House tomorrow night," she raved. "It'll be so much more fun with you there—I'll have somebody to talk to for a change! And then Saturday in Grierson I can show you all over Gran's house—especially the junk room, and—"

"Aren't you even a little bit sad about Hill leaving?" DorJo asked.

"Well, *sure* I am!"

"You act like it's not going to happen," said DorJo. "You talk about all the fun and not how sad you are."

"So?" Arden turned to her books. "There's no need to go around moaning and making everybody miserable." Nevertheless, she felt severely chastised by DorJo's quiet words, as though she'd been caught hiding from herself.

At breakfast next morning, Arden had the unmistakable feeling that some important conversation was cut short just as she and DorJo entered the kitchen. Mom and Dad seemed tired, Hill irritated. Arden and DorJo said their good mornings and slid into their places with as little fuss as possible. No one talked much. Every now and again Arden sneaked a glance around the table to see if she could get some feel for the situation, but there was no accounting for the strained atmosphere.

"What is it?" she said finally. "What's going on?"

"Well . . ." Dad began. He cleared his throat rather more than seemed necessary. "Joan and I have been talking things over." He turned to DorJo. "We've decided to inform the sheriff that you're staying with us, DorJo."

DorJo got very still. Only her eyes and mouth moved. "How come?"

"Mostly for your own protection. He needs to know that you're safe and well cared for, and that you're here by choice."

"Why'd you decide he has to know I'm here?"

"It's been nearly two weeks since you came," said Mom.

146

"If by now your mother starts thinking about looking for you, she might decide to report you missing. It wouldn't be fair to the law enforcement people to send them off on a wild-goose chase when you're right here."

"Won't the sheriff tell Mama where I am if he knows?"

"Not if we ask him not to, and explain why."

DorJo appeared to have lost her appetite. She laid her fork on the plate and put her hands in her lap.

"When she finds out I've been here all along, she's going to be mad as . . . fury. She'll tell the sheriff what I did that Friday night with the knife. She'll tell him I'm too dangerous to live with—that I ought to be in a detention home."

"You have lots of reliable character witnesses," Mom assured her. "Besides, your mother provoked you into what you did."

"It would be so much better if I went home," said DorJo. "I don't want to get Mama in trouble getting myself out of trouble."

"Look," said Dad, "if our going to the sheriff is going to make you anxious, then we won't do it."

Hill dropped his fork on the plate with a loud clank. "Well, what other choice do you have? You're already sticking your necks out keeping her here. She doesn't want to get her mother in trouble with the Law, but *you* could get sued! Does she care about that?"

Arden felt as though he'd slapped her. DorJo's eyes filled with tears but she blinked them away.

"Hill, that was uncalled for!" Dad was stern. "Apologize to DorJo."

"He don't have to do that," said DorJo. She pushed her chair back and stood up. "Excuse me. I've got to get ready for school."

"Big-mouth!" Arden hissed at him as soon as DorJo was out

of earshot. "Why'd you have to say that? She can't help what her mother does—"

"Arden!" Mom sounded very weary. "Finish your breakfast."

She stuffed the last piece of toast in her mouth and washed it down with milk, glaring at Hill the whole time. He wouldn't look at her. When she left the table she paused at the kitchen door.

"Maybe it's a good thing you're going to Grierson after all," she said angrily. "You're getting more like Grierson people every day!"

She ran upstairs before Dad could call her back to apologize.

"I don't know what's the matter with him!" she griped as she tore around the bedroom gathering up books and papers to stuff in her book pack. "If he cares so much, why's he leaving?"

DorJo didn't reply. She moved quietly, making her bed and putting away her nightclothes.

"Dor, I'm sorry. Hill is . . . is a—" She couldn't think of a word bad enough to describe him, at least not one she was allowed to say.

"Now, stop that!" DorJo said sharply. "He said what he thought. It's a free country." She went to the desk and collected her pile of homework papers, taking great care to make the edges even.

"Free doesn't mean a person has the right to hurt somebody's feelings!"

"It does, too," DorJo said reasonably. "I'm just surprised he hasn't said it out loud before now."

Arden came around the end of her bed and confronted DorJo. "Listen—don't you do something foolish just because of what Hill said. You promised Granpa Huggins you'd wait to hear from him, and you have to do that."

148

DorJo's answering look was tough and unyielding at first, but then, with a sigh, she sat down suddenly on the bed and put her hands up to her face. "I'm so mixed up. Anything I do—or don't do—just makes things worse. I wish I could disappear and everybody'd forget I ever lived."

"DorJo Huggins, if you don't stop that kind of talk, I am personally going to . . . to—" Once again at a loss for words, she sputtered to a stop. "Oh, shoot, DorJo—you give your mama too much power. We *all* do, come to think of it. She's not smarter and stronger than anyone else in Haverlee, including you. She might talk louder, but so what?"

The hands came down from DorJo's face. "A person would almost believe it, hearing you talk."

"Go ahead—believe it," Arden said. "Nothing's going to happen if Dad tells the sheriff where you are. Nothing. Things will go along just like they have been. Mom and Dad will figure out a plan this very weekend, *before* your mother starts stirring up trouble. They'll talk to Granpa and Jessie and get it all worked out. You don't have to worry."

DorJo gave a little nod and stood up. "All right—you've convinced me. I'll try not to be such a wet blanket. Come on. I've got to tell your folks it's all right for them to tell the sheriff where I am."

In the afternoon Arden, Seth, and DorJo emerged from school squinting in the sunlight. The day was gorgeous and inviting. They discussed how to spend it.

"We don't have much time," Arden told Seth. "We're all going to Porterfield to dinner tonight, so we have to be dressed and ready by six."

"Well, maybe I could come over to yours or DorJo's house for a little while," he said, brightening at the prospect.

She and DorJo exchanged worried glances. Seth still didn't

know that DorJo was living with the Giffords. "Maybe mine," Arden spoke up quickly. She realized even as she said it that Seth would wonder why they had to walk all the way around the back side of Haverlee to get home. Maybe this was the day they'd have to tell him the truth. "What do you think, Dor?"

"Sure, I—" DorJo stopped suddenly and looked beyond them to the edge of the school grounds. Arden followed her gaze. At the far corner, just across the shallow dividing ditch, stood Jessie. She was dressed in the blue nylon uniform she wore to work. Her hair was pulled back and plaited neatly in a single braid. She lifted her hand and waved.

DorJo broke into a run. Arden, once she got over her surprise, followed after, the loaded book pack thumping against her back in a most annoying manner.

"What're you doing here?" DorJo gasped, leaping over the narrow ditch. "You're supposed to be at work."

"Is that all I get from you when we haven't seen each other in days?" Jessie smiled.

A chastened DorJo shoved her notebook at Arden and ran to Jessie's outstretched arms. "I'm really glad to see you!" she said, hugging her sister tightly. "I thought . . . I didn't know if you—"

"Hush!" Jessie said firmly. She held DorJo at arm's length. She had to look up to her since DorJo was the taller of the two. "Granpa told me you and Arden came over yesterday afternoon."

"Yeah. He said he'd talk to you about us going back home. Did he?"

Arden glanced over her shoulder. Seth lingered on the school grounds, but made no attempt to come nearer. He reminded her of the horses in old western movies on TV, hanging around at the edges until he was needed again.

"That's why I came here," Jessie said. "I'm going to the plant an hour late today. Come on—I'll walk part of the way with you."

"You two go ahead," Arden said. "I have to tell Seth there's been a change of plans. I'll catch up." She scrambled back across the ditch and made her way to where he stood in a patch of shade. He had a resigned air about him, as though he already knew before she opened her mouth that the plan for the afternoon was shot.

"It's all right," he said when she told him that something unexpected had come up with DorJo's sister. "Maybe another day."

"Sure," she said. "Monday, maybe."

For a moment they stood there awkwardly. For some reason Arden thought of the snail hopscotch design painted in white on the asphalt of the teachers' parking lot. The lines of its congruent circles swirled gently inward toward the center. She saw herself and DorJo together in the center, and Seth always somewhere in the first few blocks of the outer circle.

"See ya," he said. Anxious to get back to DorJo and Jessie, Arden threw him a good-bye over her shoulder and hastened after them.

She had to run hard to catch up before they turned the corner. When she came alongside, panting and dry-mouthed, she saw first thing that DorJo was crying hard. Her wet face was all screwed out of shape. She wasn't even bothering to try to wipe the tears away. She and Jessie walked with their arms linked, but DorJo hardly seemed aware of it.

"Please try to see it from my point of view," Jessie was saying, her voice high-pitched as though she too were on the verge of tears. "When it's you and me together with her in that house, she's got me over a barrel. I end up doing things I hate because I have to take care of you."

"Like *what*?" DorJo sobbed.

"I wasn't going to tell you this," said Jessie, "but it's the only way I can get you to understand. When Mama came home this time, she and I had it out the next day while you were at school. I told her then I wasn't giving her any money—that it wasn't my place to support her and pay any debts she ran up. I told her I'd go around town and tell all the stores not to give her credit, that if she was going to stay she'd have to get a job.

" 'That's some way for a girl to treat her mother!' she said. 'Don't you have any feelings?'

" 'Don't talk to me about feelings!' " I said. 'They are not something a person turns on and off like a water faucet. If you want to be our mother, then act like one! You always pretend you haven't even been gone—do you think DorJo and me are stupid?' "

In the face of Jessie's eloquence, DorJo stopped crying. The tears dried as she listened. Arden listened, too, although she had the feeling she was in somebody else's life and had no business being there.

"She acted like I insulted her." Jessie shrugged. "Maybe so—I don't know. Far as I'm concerned, it's not an insult if it's the truth." '

"Well, it sounds like you had *her* over a barrel," said DorJo.

"Ho!" said Jessie, without mirth. "She said if I did what I said, she'd take you with her and go off somewhere and not leave any forwarding address."

"Aw, she couldn't do that!" DorJo scoffed.

"Couldn't she? She did it once years ago with both of us, and lost us our grandparents." Jessie gave DorJo a long look. DorJo dropped her head. "Mama's not dumb, DorJo. She knows you're the one misses her and wants her back. She uses it—against you, against me. I wouldn't put it past her to take you off with her one day, telling some glamorous story, and then in a week or so you'd wake up and she'd be gone with some man, and you'd be stranded in East Podunk without a cent of money or any way to get home.

"So what I'm saying, DorJo, is that I'm not going back to that place as long as she's here, and I don't want you to go back either. She puts you down, makes you feel bad about yourself, insults your friends, embarrasses you. How can you live like that? You're doing so good in school now. I don't want you to have to quit. You can be somebody if you don't have her around convincing you that you're nobody."

Arden was proud of Jessie. She was saying all the things that Arden would have said if she'd had the right to say them.

"But I feel like a sneak," said DorJo. "It's like being in prison, staying out of her sight. Arden and me can't go anywhere or do anything without being on the lookout—even walking home from school we have to go this long way. Sooner or later she'll find out, and she'll be mad. If I'm still at the Giffords she'll make trouble for them. If I go to Granpa's she might follow me there sometime and find him. It seems like the only thing to do is to go home."

"Please don't," Jessie begged. "It'll drive me crazy with worry. I promise when she leaves we'll be together again, like always. We could be together now, if you'd come to Granpa's."

"But what if she don't leave?" DorJo said. "What if this time she really means to stay. Only if we aren't there, she won't have a reason—"

Jessie shook her head. She had a sad little smile on her face. "Dor, honey, you are such a dreamer. You'd believe the best about her if she drove a bulldozer over you. I used to, but no more."

They had reached the street where Jessie had to turn. She looked at her watch. "I've got thirty minutes. It'll take me about that long to get to the plant from here." She took some money from her purse and gave it to DorJo. "This is for you. Do something fun with it." She hugged DorJo again. "Bye. Think about what I've said. I'll see you one day next week."

"Bye," said DorJo. She stood and watched her sister walk away, her eyes full of longing. Arden felt sad. On impulse she took her friend's arm and squeezed it, to let her know.

"You want to go to the hideout this afternoon?" she said.

DorJo turned and looked at her. She seemed to come back from a long distance. "No," she said, as she started walking down the street. "I don't want to go nowhere."

CHAPTER 14

ARDEN KNELT ON THE WINDOW SEAT AND LOOKED OUT OF HER bedroom window at the backyard. The maple and oak leaves were tinged with gold and pink. In another few weeks the colors would deepen until all of Haverlee would be ablaze in a quiet fire of bright, windblown leaves. She was certain that no spot in the universe could be more beautiful in autumn than right here; and yet, for DorJo, there was no beauty in it.

"Are you sure you don't want to go to the hideout, DorJo? Mom wouldn't care, so long as we got back in time to go to Porterfield."

"You go ahead. I don't feel like it." DorJo lay on her back on the bed, staring up at the ceiling.

"I already told you I never want to go there by myself again."

DorJo rolled over on her side and looked at Arden. Her forehead was creased as though her head might be hurting. "Is Jessie right?" she asked.

"I . . . don't know," Arden answered. "She sounded right, to me."

"Yeah." DorJo sighed and flopped on her back again.

Arden stood and stretched her arms high overhead. She longed to be out of doors in the fresh air, but she knew she couldn't leave DorJo alone in the house. "I left my books downstairs," she said. "I think I'll go do my homework so it won't be hanging over me all weekend. Come on down when you feel like it."

"Mmmm," DorJo said. She closed her eyes.

Arden went out, shutting the door softly behind her. The house was very still. Light coming through the narrow window at the end of the hall made rectangular patterns on the carpet. Motes of dust hung in the air like a gossamer curtain. Something in the angle of the sunlight, or perhaps it was the emptiness, made a little ache start somewhere deep inside her. Instead of going directly downstairs, she went along the hall to Hill's room. The door stood open. The floor was covered with cardboard boxes, some already taped shut, others half-filled with books, record albums, and mementos. His suitcase lay open on a table. The walls, once covered with posters, were stripped bare. The bookcase was empty of all except a few volumes. Hill's rumpled, unmade bed seemed to be the last tangible evidence of him, the person. Already he was becoming like a ghost.

When the doorbell chimed suddenly, she was startled. People seldom came calling at this hour because everyone knew her parents worked. Partly because she was feeling so lonely, she ran down the stairs and flung open the door without peering through one of the panes of glass first to see who the caller was. Immediately she was sorry.

There, big as life, right on her own front porch, was Mrs. Huggins.

"Oh!" said Arden, feeling the breath leave her lungs. Her first impulse was to slam the door and lock it, but she had

156

enough presence of mind to know that wouldn't do. "H— hello."

"I want to speak to your Ma," Mrs. Huggins said without preliminary.

"Sh . . . she's not home from work yet," Arden said, clutching the doorknob.

"What time does she get home?"

"Usually about five thirty. She works in Porterfield at the hospital lab." She prayed silently that DorJo wouldn't hear.

Mrs. Huggins didn't go away. The brown sweater she wore over her pink dress was too tight for her arms. Her hands, stuffed into the pockets, stretched it downward out of shape. She did not look mean today.

"I have been thinking DorJo and Jessie was together all this time," Mrs. Huggins said. "I went to the chicken plant yesterday to talk to Jessie, but the foreman said she wouldn't come out to see me. I don't know where she spends her nights— there's no tellin'."

All the time she was talking, Mrs. Huggins was looking straight into Arden's eyes. Arden's mind flitted about like a frightened caged bird. She thought she heard a door open upstairs and all the blood rushed to her heart.

"So . . . y . . . you think that DorJo isn't with Jessie?" was all she could manage.

The woman sighed. It was a great, gusty sigh, the sort that a person makes when they've done everything they've thought of doing and it doesn't work. "*I* don't know," she said. "I thought—"

She stopped, closing her lips firmly over whatever she had been going to say.

"I guess you . . . must be worried about DorJo," Arden said, not really believing it, but at a loss for something to say that wouldn't give away secrets.

"Well, of *course* I'm worried!" Mrs. Huggins's eyes reddened. "She's not but twelve years old—if you was such a good friend, you'd be worried, too!"

"Yes," said Arden. Her lips felt stiff, as on a very cold day. "Where've you looked for her?"

"Where *would* I look, for God's sake? Behind bushes? Under houses? Where does a young'un go when she runs away? I don't know!"

"Maybe she's afraid to come home," said Arden.

The woman regarded her as though she were from a foreign country. "Now, why would she be afraid to come home?"

Arden swallowed, trying to separate what she knew from what she was supposed to know. "Well . . . from what you said last Monday when I went by your house . . . it sounded like you were mad at her when she left."

"So? Haven't your folks ever been mad at you?"

"Yes'm, but—"

"Did you run away?"

"No." The argument was not going well. She wanted to shout, "But my parents are fair! They wouldn't threaten me!" To risk insulting Mrs. Huggins, however, would do no good at all. Arden didn't feel very heroic.

"Well, then," said Mrs. Huggins, as if that settled it. She took her hands out of the pockets and made as if to button the sweater, although it wasn't at all cold. Her next question was completely unexpected. "Where do you think she is?"

Oh, help, thought Arden. Her knees were jelly. A trickle of sweat ran down her side. She felt it under her shirt. Never good at lying, she picked her way through possible answers like a barefoot person walks around broken glass. "Well, I . . . looked in places I thought she would be."

"Was she there?"

"No, ma'am," she said, thankful that she could say it truthfully. After all, DorJo had found *them*, not the other way around.

Mrs. Huggins's shoulders slumped a little. "I was hoping you'd know something." She looked off down the street, one hand on her hip, the other hanging limply by her side. Arden saw a tremor of the woman's chin, the stretching of lips as when a person tries to hold back tears. Mrs. Huggins was probably not one to weep in front of people—she was too tough.

Arden felt dreadful. How could she justify not telling Mrs. Huggins what she needed to know? She had a responsibility to many people to keep it a secret for now, and yet . .

Then she remembered how Mrs. Huggins had acted the day she, Arden, was so worried about DorJo—mean and unconcerned. Why should Mrs. Huggins expect Arden to be helpful now?

"Maybe you should come back when my folks are home," she said.

Mrs. Huggins shrugged and turned to go. "If you don't know anything, they probably don't either. Thanks anyway." There was no sullenness in her tone, just resignation.

Arden watched until Mrs. Huggins reached the sidewalk, then closed the door. She stood for a minute or more holding onto the doorknob, not sure she could trust herself to move from the spot. She looked at her Timex. It was an hour before Mom would be home. She listened. The upstairs silence was undisturbed. She must have imagined, in her fright, the opening door.

She wandered into the kitchen and walked around in it, going from sink to refrigerator to cabinet without really thinking what she was doing or why. The enormity of what she had done had so stunned her that she couldn't hold on to one thought long enough to connect it to another. In her mind she followed Mrs. Huggins down the street, wondering where the woman would go now.

Gradually, in the stillness, she became calmer, but with the calmness came a sick feeling. She began to think through what would happen when she told Mom and Dad about the afternoon visitor. She knew exactly what they would do—get into the car and go straight over to the Huggins house. Hill's last-night-home party would go up in smoke. And, of course, if she told DorJo, there would be no second thoughts so far as her friend was concerned—she'd gather up her belongings and go home, regardless of what Jessie or anyone said.

Arden did not trust Mrs. Huggins to treat DorJo kindly. Why couldn't she at least have waited until the weekend was over? She certainly hadn't made any huge effort to find DorJo before now. Why let her mess up all the plans they'd made?

Well, she thought, I am the only one who knows Mrs. Huggins came this afternoon. If I don't tell, then things will go along as planned. Sunday is soon enough.

Somehow, though, the decision did not bring her any relief. She kept seeing Mrs. Huggins's face, the way it looked when hope left it.

"She should've been worried before now!" she said aloud, but it sounded like so much big talk in the empty air.

The unmistakable sound of a VW engine coming into the driveway made her heart leap. Hill was home!

When she burst out of the door and threw herself at him, he was just emerging backward from under the hood of his car with an armload of books. Taken unawares, he dropped them all over the driveway.

"For pete's sake, Aardvark—what's going on!" he yelled. "Look what you did!"

"Sorry!" she said in a small voice. "I was just glad you were home. I'll pick 'em up." She bent hastily and began picking up books, dusting each one and straightening mashed pages.

"Are you O.K.?" he asked in a much milder tone. She looked up at him, sorry for the secret she had to hold.

"Sure!" she said with forced brightness. "I had forgotten you didn't have to work today. Having you home early is . . . is great."

Hill studied her with narrowed eyes. "If I didn't know better, I'd think I had caught you with your hand in the cookie jar."

She put on a great show of indignation. "I'll drop all these books again if you keep that up. Can't a person be glad to see her own brother without him making a federal case of it?"

"Well, sure. But you have to admit it's quite a change of attitude from this morning."

She hung her head. "That was pretty awful, what I said to you. I wasn't being fair. DorJo said you were right."

He took some of the books from her and they went inside together. "No, I wasn't right. One of the first things I intend to do this afternoon is to apologize to DorJo. I hurt her feelings. No excuses."

"She didn't take it as bad as I did," Arden said. "Maybe she's more used to having her feelings hurt."

"People shouldn't have to get used to it," Hill said. He put the books on the kitchen counter and made a beeline for the refrigerator. "I had a fit of jealousy."

"Jealousy! What for?" She pulled out a chair and sat down. He began putting the ingredients for a sandwich out on the table.

"Well, it's the eve of my departure, and what's my family all concerned about? DorJo Huggins." He gave her a shame-faced look. "I got moved out of the spotlight, see."

She admired him tremendously for saying it out loud. She didn't think she could have done it if she had been in his place. "You have a right to be jealous," she said warmly, feeling somewhat better for her decision. "You ought to have the spotlight! DorJo understands that. It's why she took it so well."

"I didn't want to leave with you and me on bad terms," he said, grinning at her. He set about making the sandwich. She watched him, comforted by his presence and by the support his admission of jealousy gave her to keep her mouth shut about Mrs. Huggins's visit.

"By the way," he said, looking around, "where is DorJo? I've hardly seen the two of you apart since she came here."

"Upstairs. We met Jessie on the way home from school, and Jessie kind of laid down the law—told her not to go back home as long as her mother was there." She sighed. "DorJo wants them to be a family again so much. She feels really down right now. When we got home she didn't want to do anything but lie on the bed and look at the ceiling."

"Do you think she'll be in the mood for a party tonight?" he asked.

"Oh, sure—she'll feel better by now." She looked at the rooster clock over the refrigerator. "I guess I'd better go up and remind her. Mom'll want us to leave here pretty soon after six."

"I want to tell DorJo I'm sorry for what I said this morning," Hill told her.

"All right." She smiled at him, but it felt kind of shaky because all of a sudden she was thinking he wouldn't be here tomorrow night or any other night after this except for visits. She left the kitchen quickly, to keep from thinking.

She wished that the staircase had one hundred steps, to give her time to prepare for what she was going to do. At the same time, she knew she could never have enough time to get ready. She and DorJo had always trusted each other. She felt the secret like a lie branded on her face.

With a fearful and guilty heart she opened the bedroom door and peeped in. DorJo still lay on the bed, her head turned the other way. "Dor?" she said softly.

DorJo rolled over and faced her, squinting slightly, as though her eyes were not used to being open. "What time is it?"

"Close to six o'clock. You must've been asleep." Arden came into the room and sat down on the end of the bed. "Feel better?"

DorJo stretched and yawned, rubbing at her eyes to get them open. "I guess so. Kind of gray. When I first woke up, I felt that way and couldn't think why. Then I remembered." She sat up slowly, crossing her legs Indian style, and peered at Arden. "What's up?"

Arden swallowed. "Nothing. Hill's home. Mom and Dad will be home in a few minutes. Don't forget we're going to eat in Porterfield tonight."

The expression on DorJo's face didn't change, but she looked at Arden a moment longer, as though something puzzled her. Then she shrugged and got off the bed.

"Do we have to dress up?"

"Just skirt and sweater," Arden said, thankful the moment had passed.

"I don't have any business going out with you and your folks tonight," DorJo said, opening her side of the closet and peering into it. She didn't seem to remember why she was there. "I'd rather stay here. I feel like a extra leg or something."

"Well, you're not an extra leg. You're my best friend. I want you to be with us tonight, and I want you to go to Grierson tomorrow, too, because I hate that place. The only reason I'm looking forward to it this time is because you'll be there and I can show you places and have you meet Gran and Big Dad."

Why am I talking so much? she wondered, feeling like two people instead of one. She got up and went to the closet, too.

"We can be twins," she said. "Let's both wear our plaid skirts and green sweaters."

DorJo snorted. "How can you make twins out of a bear and a deer? Look-alike clothes sure won't do it!" The notion amused her. Her mood lightened some, so that during the time they spent getting ready, Arden was able to relax a little.

But the evening put her severely to the test. Riding over to Porterfield, she, DorJo, and Hill sat in the backseat. Hill made his apology to DorJo in a humble and gentlemanly way.

"Look," she said, obviously uncomfortable, "just forget it. I don't blame you for being upset—if I was in your place I'd be boiling. You don't need to be sorry for what you said."

"But I am," Hill persisted. "I acted like a baby."

"Well, all right then," said DorJo, and that was the end of it. She seemed to be determined that Hill should get his due on this last night home.

Arden looked out of the car window a lot, her mind still back in Haverlee. She imagined Mrs. Huggins coming over to their darkened house and discovering that they were gone. Perhaps she would sit on the porch until they came home, and when she saw DorJo she would let them all have it with a barrage of fury. That's when Mom and Dad—and DorJo— would find out about the earlier visit, and everyone would turn on Arden. Maybe if they stayed in Porterfield long enough Mrs. Huggins would lose patience and go home.

"You sure aren't talking much," DorJo observed. "Are you mad at me?"

"Oh, no!" Arden was dismayed that she might have given DorJo that impression. "I was just . . . thinking."

After that she tried to be more sociable, but several times during the evening she caught her mind crawling away in its own direction. She wanted so much to be rid of the burden of her secret. It seemed to her that the words lay on the back of her tongue like an undissolved pill, ready to roll out whenever she opened her mouth. For that reason she was more careful than usual about speaking up. Mostly she watched and listened to everyone else.

Hill kept everyone laughing with his clever imitations of teachers. Dad obligingly played straight man, to make it funnier. For all the hilarity, though, Arden sensed a kind of desperation among all of them, herself included. Once in a while, in the glow of the candles on their table, she saw Mom's eyes glisten. Occasionally there would be a lull in the conversation. When this happened they would not look at each other. Instead, someone would comment on the food.

The condemned ate a hearty meal.

The words popped into her head unbidden. She laid her fork upon the plate carefully, feeling that if she did anything suddenly, something would break or tear.

"Arden, honey, I do believe you're coming down with something," Mom said. "You've left so much food on your plate, and you're as pasty as a raw potato."

"Yuk!" Hill said. "That's an awful simile after such a great meal."

"Hush!" Mom told him, not taking her eyes off of Arden. "What is it, Arden? Do you feel bad?"

Yes, I feel horrible, she thought, very close to putting her head on the linen tablecloth and bawling the words.

"No, I'm fine," she said aloud in a thin little voice. "Really."

Mom continued to frown. "Maybe you'd better not plan to go to Grierson tomorrow."

"I'm all right!" Arden said emphatically. Everyone got very quiet. Then Hill changed the subject and everyone began talking brightly again, as though nothing had happened. DorJo, however, gave her another of those long, steady looks.

This must be what a giant clam feels like when an octopus

is trying to get it open, Arden thought despairingly.

On the way home she sat by the window again and looked up at the stars. She imagined herself among them, looking down at this car speeding along the highway toward Haverlee. Well, not really speeding, but going back much faster than she would have liked. It was scarcely nine thirty. Mrs. Huggins might even now be sitting on their porch, waiting.

"Arden, you are acting funny," DorJo said next to her ear. "What *is* it?"

"It's just Hill's leaving and all," she whispered back. DorJo's look of sympathy made her feel all the more terrible.

Oh, Dor, she thought, her eyes filling with tears. You are going to hate me so! Blinking furiously, she turned toward the window again. For the first time in her recent life, she wished they were already in Grierson.

CHAPTER 15

ACCORDING TO THE PLAN, HILL WAS TO DRIVE THE VW TO GRIER-
son. The rest of the bags, boxes, and people would be loaded
into the larger car.

It was barely light outside when the five of them sat down
to breakfast on Saturday morning. Mom was still in her
housecoat.

"DorJo and I will clean up the kitchen so you can get ready,"
Arden said to her. Somehow she had a strong need to please
everyone today, to be extra nice.

"I'm not going," said Mom. The calm words were like a
bombshell.

Hill set his glass down with a thump. "Not going? But,
Mom—"

"I'm not. That's all there is to it."

"But why?" Arden asked. "Is it because there isn't enough
room for all of us? If that's it, DorJo and I will stay here." But
even as she said it, she could feel dread like sludge moving
along her veins. She didn't want to stay here alone today with

DorJo, harboring her secret like it was some infectious disease. And what if Mrs. Huggins came back?

"There's plenty of room for anyone who wants to go," Dad said. He didn't seem surprised at Mom's announcement. Arden figured they had talked it over already.

"At the risk of sounding like a baby," Mom said, "I just don't think I can take it. If I go I'll have to act cheerful and wonderful. Since that's not how I feel, I'd just as soon tell you good-bye this morning, Hill, and have the rest of the day to get over it."

"I'm just going to Grierson, Mom!"

"I know—thank goodness. I'll still miss you, though. I'd miss you even if you were just moving across town. Don't stew about it—this is just something I need to do. I'll start early—clean the house like a fiend. By the time Dad and the girls get home tonight, I'll be fine."

"Yes," said Dad. "We'll come home sniveling about five o'clock and you'll have to comfort *us*."

Hill's face showed his disappointment, and his sadness. "Look, are you all trying to make me feel bad or something? I don't want to leave *you*—it's scary, going to a new place where I hardly know anyone but Gran and Big Dad. I wish you wouldn't make it worse!"

Dad's mouth twitched. He looked at Mom with a twinkle in his eye. "Want to change your mind?"

"No," said Mom, lifting her chin a little. "Absolutely not. Now, hurry up. All that stuff has to be loaded into the cars before anyone goes anywhere."

Nearly an hour later the two cars rolled out of the driveway packed to the limit with suitcases, boxes, odd-shaped bundles, tennis rackets, baseball paraphernalia, and a battered guitar. Hill drove ahead, with Dad's express orders not to exceed the speed limit. DorJo and Arden were separated from each other

168

on the backseat of the other car by a large, soft wedge of sleeping bag and pillow. Their last view was of Mom leaning halfway out the front door, holding her housecoat shut with one hand and waving good-bye with the other.

For the first few miles the three of them were quiet, too sleepy or too pensive to talk. Arden studied the back of Dad's head, the way the faintly visible lines on his neck crisscrossed each other like webs. That set her to thinking about when people started having lines on their skin, and whether one day the skin's surface was smooth and then the very next day the etching had begun.

"Somehow or other I'd expected the backseat to sound like a squirrel convention," Dad said suddenly. "What's the matter?"

"Nothing," said Arden. "I was just thinking."

"And I was just looking," said DorJo, turning away from the window. She had been staring out of it ever since they left Haverlee. "Porterfield is the furtherest I've been since we moved to Haverlee. We never had no way to go anywhere."

"Well," said Arden, "I have been to lots of places, but Haverlee is the best. I'd rather live there than anywhere in the world."

DorJo looked out of the window again. "I don't know if I think that," she said. "I don't 'specially want to spend the rest of my days in Haverlee."

"You sound like Hill," Arden said, half-joking, yet feeling a faint sense of betrayal. She could sort of understand how DorJo felt since she'd never had the adventure of travel, but for herself, leaving Haverlee would be like leaving a person she loved. She looked quickly out of the window at her once undersea world, now abandoned to air and sky. Perhaps anyone who craved excitement would find it too placid and flat. Right now DorJo couldn't seem to get enough of looking, but it wasn't so much what was there that engaged her attention as what might suddenly turn up on the landscape—something different or spectacular. For Arden its attraction was just the opposite—the constancy, the unchangeableness of the land was what she loved so much.

"It used to be under the ocean, you know," she said.

DorJo turned in the seat to stare at her. "What are you talking about?"

"Mom told me—the coastal plain used to be under the ocean. It's been dry land for less than a hundred thousand years."

Dad chuckled. "Practically yesterday, in cosmic terms."

"You don't have to make fun," Arden said. "It's not so long ago, when you think about the billions of years before that!"

"You're right," he apologized. "It's just that . . . a lot can happen in a hundred thousand years."

"Or even ten years," DorJo said soberly. She took a deep breath and let it out slowly. "One hundred thousand makes me dizzy."

Hill's VW stayed a consistent and respectable distance in front of them all the way to Grierson. In what seemed no time at all they were entering the city. This time, though, they arrived before the traffic began to clot the streets. Few people were out. Grierson had a clean, uncluttered look this early in the morning. Once again Arden felt betrayed, this time because the city itself seemed to be deliberately enticing her to see it with different eyes.

I don't like you. She folded her arms adamantly, sure that the city's great silent mind knew exactly what she was thinking. And you can't make me.

"Wow!" DorJo said in almost reverent tones. "Look at those tall buildings! I bet they rock back and forth when the wind blows."

"It's true—they do," Dad said. "They're built that way. I'm

told by people who work in them that you can feel the sway on a very windy day."

"Ugh!" said Arden. "Just thinking about that makes me sick."

"I don't know." DorJo had a new light in her eye. "Maybe it would be fun."

By the time they reached the house on Talley Street, Arden was already beginning to wonder whether bringing DorJo to Grierson was such a good idea after all. The trouble was, people got fooled by all the things to look at and do. They didn't know there was more to life than that . . . things like having close neighbors and knowing everybody's name.

Hill had already pulled into the driveway ahead of them and had unfolded himself from under the wheel of the VW. Gran and Big Dad came bursting out of the front door as though they had been waiting just inside it since the last visit.

DorJo hung back during the hugging and kissing. She smiled, but her eyes were anxious.

"And this is Arden's friend, DorJo Huggins," said Dad, taking her by the arm and leading her forward. "DorJo, this is my father and my mother, Mr. and Mrs. Gifford."

"Hello, DorJo," Gran said, smiling as she shook DorJo's hand. "I'm glad you came along."

"So am I," Big Dad boomed, holding DorJo's hand in both of his big ones. Arden thought that for a change her friend must feel like a pygmy. "Any pal of Arden's is welcome to the family."

This time DorJo's smile went all the way to her eyes. "Thanks," she said, bobbing her head a little.

There was some discussion of Mom's absence and why, then everyone took part of Hill's stuff and followed Gran inside. Arden, at the rear of the line, watched the others preceding her up the great staircase, thinking that they really were like a safari she had seen on television toiling up a mountainside. Gran was calling out orders and the rest of them were lugging packs and bundles.

"Here's your new home, Hill," Gran said, standing at the door and gesturing with one hand. "Your dad's old room."

"Hey, now!" Dad said, pretending to be upset. "I didn't say you could—"

"Tom, hush!" Gran scolded. "You've been gone too long to have any more say about who sleeps in these rooms!"

Arden giggled at the feigned tremble of Dad's lips. He acted so silly! Hill made a big deal of putting his arm across Dad's shoulders and saying, "There, there—don't cry!"

It took two trips with everyone helping to bring up the last of Hill's possessions. When it was done, the once-orderly room resembled earthquake city. Gran looked worried. Maybe, thought Arden, she was just beginning to remember how it used to be with teenage boys in the house.

"Well, now," Gran said, smoothing her hands along her skirt front. "I suggest we leave everything right where it is for the time being. Hill can spend tomorrow putting things where he wants them." She turned to Arden. "Why don't I telephone for Liz and Teresa to come over? The four of you could have Cokes and cookies in the summerhouse."

Arden flashed an anxious look at Dad, but he was talking to Big Dad and didn't see. "Well, I'd rather not," she said. "I mean, since it's DorJo's first visit here, I just kind of wanted to show her around. I thought perhaps—if it was okay with you—I could show her the attic junk room and—"

"Oh, for heaven's sake, Arden!" Gran threw up her hands and laughed, but it didn't sound like a real laugh to Arden. It had an irritated edge to it. "The junk room? Dear, I thought you'd outgrown that sort of thing by now!"

Taken aback, Arden merely looked at Gran, waiting for the

moment to pass. Gran had never before objected to her exploration of the house.

"Oh, well." Gran shrugged. "If that's what you want to do. But be sure to put things back when you get through with them."

"Yes, ma'am." Arden felt hurt. She had never in all her life failed to return each item to its proper place. Quite the opposite, she had always felt that she was the special guardian of the relics of past days that were now housed in the junk room. Part of her was convinced that it was only her attention and admiration that kept them from crumbling away to nothing.

During this exchange DorJo stood to one side looking ill at ease. She seemed relieved when the grown-ups went back downstairs and Arden began the grand tour.

The blue bedroom was the first stop. "This is where we'll sleep when we come up to visit Hill," Arden said, thoroughly satisfied with DorJo's obvious appreciation of the room's elegance.

"We, who?" DorJo asked in a hushed voice as they stood just inside the doorway.

"You and I, of course!"

"I doubt I'll come with you," DorJo said.

"Sure you will! Why not?"

"Your Gran don't like me." Her tone was matter-of-fact and held no rancor, but Arden was shocked all the same.

"That's silly, DorJo! She doesn't even know you—we haven't even been here thirty minutes!"

"I can tell. It's all right, though—she don't have to like me." DorJo began moving around the room, examining the satin comforter, running her hand over its rich smoothness, looking at herself in the large mirror.

Arden couldn't let it go. "I think you're wrong," she said,

following DorJo about. She had intended to point out the huge wardrobe in the corner with its double doors, and the old-fashioned desk on spindly legs that had more little drawers and poky holes than you could count and a drawer that opened with a secret spring. All that was forgotten, though, in light of this new development. "Gran was a schoolteacher. She likes kids! You'll see when we get to the junk room. I mean, a person who didn't like kids would never save all that neat stuff."

"I'm not saying your Gran don't like kids," DorJo said patiently. "It's me she has trouble with. Maybe she thinks I'm not good enough to be your friend. But it's all right, and I wish you wouldn't keep on talking about it. I'm not going to be here but just today."

How could she keep from talking about it? Arden wondered as she led DorJo through the rest of the upstairs. The matter hung in the air as real and as obtrusive as the presence of one of the town girls.

At the rear of the upstairs hall was the narrow little door to the attic staircase. Arden had dreamed for days of the exciting moment when she would take DorJo to this most special of places, but now the dream had lost its warmth. "The attic's up these little steps," she said, and beckoned DorJo to follow. "It might be stuffy up here."

Soon the two of them were standing in the attic, which ran the length of the house. It smelled of mothballs, cedar, old paper, dried wood, wax, and a number of other unidentifiable odors that all ran together. Ancient trunks were piled up in the slanting portion under the eaves. In the middle section, where they could stand upright, were shabby pieces of furniture that Gran intended to fix someday, bundles of magazines dating back five decades, metal phonograph records, Uncle Bob's and Dad's old toys, out-of-fashion clothes, even books and art supplies from Gran's years of teaching.

174

A slight breeze blew between the vents, making it bearable in spite of the day's warmth. October and April were usually the best months for playing in the attic. Arden pulled a string and the single bare bulb cast its inadequate light in the attic's midsection.

"Well, here it is," she said.

It was impossible to tell from DorJo's expression what she thought. She looked around without moving from the spot where she stood. "Sure is a lot of stuff," she commented finally. "How come they keep all this?"

"Well, it's . . . it's from all the years of their life," Arden tried to explain. "When they were young, and when Dad and Uncle Bob were babies, and then growing up." Her words seemed to her to meander like a stream that has lost its bed. She was not prepared for DorJo's indifference. She had been so sure that the sight of the rag dolls sitting in a child's rocker, Gran's tiny china tea set, and the rack of yellowing evening gowns would delight her friend as much as they delighted her.

DorJo took a deep breath and wrinkled her nose. "Smells kind of funny up here, don't it?"

"I guess so," Arden said, "but I like it." She went over to the little cabinet that held Gran's tea set and squatted down beside it. She opened the glass doors carefully, as Gran had taught her to do. "Here—look at this. Gran had it when she was a little girl. Her big brother brought it to her from England after World War I."

DorJo came over but she remained standing. "It's pretty," she said noncommitally. Arden closed the cabinet without taking out any of the dishes. She rose and went to the rack where the old clothes hung.

"Look at this," she said, taking down a long maroon velvet dress. "Gran wore this on her honeymoon in the nineteen thirties. She lets me play dress-up in it if I'm careful."

"It's too hot for that," DorJo said, making a fanning motion with her hand.

Arden returned the velvet dress to the rack. "Is there anything you see you'd like to look at up close?" she asked.

"Not 'specially." DorJo looked toward the top of the stairs. "Fresh air is what I'd like the most."

"Oh. Well . . . all right." Arden could not keep the disappointment out of her voice. "Maybe we can come up again later, after you've seen the rest of the house."

"Mmmm," DorJo replied, already on her way down the steps.

Arden followed reluctantly, her heart still in the attic among her treasures. They were her main reason for coming to Grierson anymore. The excitement this time had come from the prospect of sharing them with DorJo. She wanted so much to look at the things, to handle them, to arrange and rearrange them, to imagine their beginnings, their newness. But it wasn't what DorJo wanted to do.

They went all over the house in what seemed to her an awfully short time. Gran, fussing about in the kitchen, gave them a distracted smile when they came through and said, "Now, you just make yourselves at home, girls," as though she didn't have time to worry about them. They went out into the huge backyard. The round summerhouse had always been one of Arden's refuges, particularly in recent years. Its open trelliswork let the sun in, but it also held the wisteria vines whose leaves gave shade. It contained a double wooden glider with facing seats that had served her as a train, a plane, a spaceship—even as a cradle. DorJo's eyes lit up.

"Can we sit in it?" she asked.

"Sure! The only rule is not to swing too high."

They sat opposite each other, swinging back and forth. Strangely, Arden found it hard to think of anything to say.

176

DorJo seemed restless. She put her feet up on Arden's side of the glider and stared out through the arched entrance into the yard beyond.

"How far is it to downtown from here?" she asked.

Arden shrugged. "I don't know for sure—I've never walked it. Maybe three miles."

DorJo grinned. "You want let's walk it now?"

Arden stared. "You mean, walk all the way downtown? In Grierson? Gran would have a fit!"

The animation in DorJo's eyes died. She made a face. "What's the good of being in a city like this if you just stay cooped up in a yard all the time?"

"Aw, Grierson's just big—it's not all that great."

"I wish Mama could come here," DorJo said after a minute or two.

"She probably already has," Arden said tactlessly, not really thinking of the effect her words would have. "She's traveled a lot . . ."

DorJo's silence was a judgment. Everything came back to Arden in a rush—Mrs. Huggins' visit, the half-truths that she, Arden had told, the chasm of deceit between her and DorJo. She felt miserable. She leaned back and closed her eyes. Drowsiness crept up her arms and legs. The sleeplessness of the night before and the morning's early rising took their toll. She heard the monotonous squeak of the glider in motion, and then at some point she didn't hear it anymore.

CHAPTER 16

SHE STRUGGLED AWAKE TO THE SOUND OF GRAN CALLING, "ARDEN! Oh, Ar-den! Come inside and help me get dinner on the table!"

She sprang up almost before her eyes were open, dazed by sleep and not absolutely sure where she was. For an instant she braced herself with one hand against the glider frame, feeling the rough wood beneath her fingers.

Then she remembered DorJo. She looked all about, but saw no sign of her friend. Well, perhaps she had already gone in to help Gran. Maybe they were on better terms now.

"Ar-den!"

"I'm coming!" she answered, stepping onto the grass. "Right now!"

She heard the back screen door slam and wondered if she was imagining its impatient sound. Still looking about for DorJo, she crossed the yard to the back porch. The marvelous smells of Gran's cooking washed over her the instant she stepped inside. Half-smiling, she thought about DorJo eating one of

Gran's dinners. That should spark her enthusiasm, all right! Even though she was sure that DorJo had imagined Gran's dislike of her, the meal should cure any doubts. DorJo would love the food and she would say so, and Gran would warm up to her because she always liked it when people appreciated her cooking.

Gran was scurrying around the kitchen in that last great moment when all the food is getting done at once and having to be taken out of the oven or transferred from pots to serving bowls.

"The table isn't set yet, Arden. Quick—get in there and put the plates and silver around."

"Yes, ma'am." She felt chastised. Gran would have liked it for her to come in earlier and volunteer. Usually she did that when she came to Grierson alone.

"Where's your friend?" Gran called to her while she was setting the table. "Did you get tired of each other?"

"No, ma'am." Gran's question angered her—did she want them to be tired of each other?

"Well, where is she?"

"Outside," Arden answered vaguely. There was no reply from the kitchen. In a moment Gran came into the dining room and surveyed the table.

"Nice," she said. "You can call the menfolk and DorJo to dinner. Show her where to wash up."

The "menfolk" in the living room were involved in a heated discussion about national politics. Arden noted that Hill was talking as much as Dad and Big Dad. It gave her a little lost feeling that he was crossing over to being one of "them."

"Dinner's ready," she said, barely sticking her head in the door. She didn't wait to see whether they'd stop talking and head for the dining room, but went straight outside. The sun overhead was very bright and she shaded her eyes with her hand.

"DorJo!" she called. "Dinner's ready!"

A breeze rattled the stiff magnolia leaves. Arden fancied that the tree was trying to tell her where DorJo had gone. She began to walk around the yard, calling and calling. At first she was puzzled, then worried, and finally angry. At least five minutes had passed. Gran would not like this at all. She and the others would be seated at the table, waiting.

She went to the end of the front walk and leaned out to look up and down the street. To her astonishment, she saw DorJo's unmistakable figure coming toward her from about two blocks away.

Just then the front door opened. "Arden, for pete's sake, come on—Gran's about to have a fit!" Hill called.

"You all go ahead and start. DorJo's way down the street. No telling when she'll get here. Just don't wait for us."

"What's she doing down the street?"

"I don't know! Just go ahead."

He shrugged and went back inside. By this time DorJo had crossed to their block. Arden ran to meet her.

"Where were you?" She knew she sounded cross, but she couldn't help it. "I've been calling you for ages! Gran has dinner on the table and they're waiting for us."

"Sorry," DorJo said. "I went for a walk. I guess I should've told somebody, but you were asleep. It seemed a shame to come all the way here and not do anything but sit in a swing all day."

"What if you had gotten lost?" Arden fussed. "You've never been here before. You could've taken a wrong turn and the next thing you—"

"I was paying attention," DorJo said calmly. "I knew where I was."

By this time they were in front of the house. Arden sighed. "Well, we have some explaining to do. Gran doesn't like for people to be late for meals."

As soon as the words were out of her mouth she regretted them. She hadn't explained Gran's rules to DorJo. How was she to know?

"I said I was sorry, didn't I?" DorJo said. "I *am*. What can I do about it now, except to tell your gran I'm sorry, I won't do it again. I won't *be* here to do it again."

"Oh, shoot! It's my fault for going to sleep like I did." Arden was contrite. "Forget what I said."

DorJo didn't say anything. They washed their hands and then came to the table, fifteen minutes late. Gran's expression was just on the edge of severe. Dad's eyebrows went up slightly, but he didn't ask any questions.

"We're sorry," Arden said, grasping the back of the chair where she was supposed to sit. "I forgot to tell DorJo when dinner would be ready—and I went to sleep in the glider."

"No, it's my fault," DorJo said. "I went for a walk downtown and didn't keep track of the time."

"Downtown?" Big Dad was amazed. "You mean from here? Aren't you tired?"

DorJo's expression softened a bit. "Not too."

"Well, you're here now," Gran said brusquely. "Sit down, both of you, I'll serve your plates."

"What did you see?" Dad asked DorJo. "Anything worth reporting?"

"Lots of things," she answered. "It was . . . inter'sting. But I expect you have seen it all before."

"I should've thought about taking you down myself," he said.

DorJo shook her head. "Thanks, but it wouldn't have been right for you to do that today." She glanced over at Hill as she

accepted the laden plate that Gran passed to her. She unfolded
the linen napkin and put it in her lap. Her intention seemed
to be to make herself invisible.

Conversation resumed but the girls didn't take part in it.
Soon Arden was aware that the others were ready for their
dessert, but were waiting for them to get through. She felt
Gran's impatience. She sighed inwardly and wished with all
her heart that they had not come today. Even the prospect of
facing Mrs. Huggins wouldn't have been as bad as this.

Arden and DorJo tried to make amends for being late by
helping Gran with the cleaning up after dinner. DorJo was
almost grim, as though she knew she not only hadn't passed
Gran's test but never would. Still, she handled the precious
dishes with great care and worked steadily and uncomplain-
ingly until the last one was put away. Gran didn't talk much.
When Arden visited alone, she and Gran had great conver-
sations, just like two grown-ups—or two kids. But with DorJo
along, it was as though Gran had made them into strangers
to whom she would be polite, but that was all. It was on the
tip of Arden's tongue to come right out and ask Gran what
was bothering her, but she didn't. Either Gran would say
nothing was bothering her, or she would tell the truth. Arden
wasn't sure she was ready to hear either answer.

Dad came into the kitchen as they were finishing.

"Well, girls, I think we'd better head back for Haverlee.
Hill needs to start getting used to his new life without us
hanging around."

Arden felt slightly sick. It was really true—they were leaving
Hill here. He wouldn't be home when they returned there.

"Maybe you'd like to go tell him good-bye, Arden," Dad
said gently

She swallowed. "Yes, sir."

"I think he's upstairs in his room."

She went out of the kitchen without looking at any of them. Her face felt exposed. She could not control the way it looked. All the little muscles around her mouth felt loose and trembly. She was going to cry in spite of everything—she just knew it. She climbed the stairs, her eyes wide and unblinking to hold the tears back as long as possible. The door to Hill's room stood open.

"Hill?" she called in a thin voice, even before she got to the top of the stairs.

"Yes?" came the muffled reply. He sounded like he was under something.

"Dad says it's time for us to go home," she said, walking along the hall. Then she was at the door to his room, looking in. He was standing by the window. "I came to say good-bye."

He came over to her. His eyes were a little bit red, as though he might have been crying, too. "Bye, Aardvark," he said, pulling her close to him. "I'm gonna miss you."

She just looked up at him because she couldn't say a word. Tears gathered and blurred her vision. Her nose began to run. She swallowed and swallowed, trying to get her voice back.

"Will you come back home sometimes?" she asked finally, when she was able.

"Sure. I'll have to, to give Gran and Big Dad a break." He patted her shoulder awkwardly. "And you'll have to come here, too. Promise?"

She hesitated, because she didn't really want to come back here, especially after this day. But she did want to see Hill. It would be selfish not to come back.

She nodded. Standing on tiptoe she gave him a quick peck on the cheek, something she hadn't done in years and years. With a small shock she felt the stubble of his beard against her lips. Of course she knew he shaved, but somehow, until that very moment it had not seemed real to her that Hill had truly gone over to the other side where people were serious and adult.

With a little wave, she turned and went out. Straight downstairs and out the front door she went. She did not want to talk to anyone. All that business of standing around and telling Gran and Big Dad good-bye, forget it! She opened the back door of the now-empty car and crawled in, slamming it behind her. She sat in the corner of the rear seat, her back toward the house and her knees drawn up, waiting.

After a while she heard voices and the sounds of footsteps on the porch, but she did not turn around. She closed her eyes, pretending, as she had done when she was very young, that no one could see her.

A fingernail rapped on the window behind her head. "Arden?" said Dad. "Aren't you going to tell Gran and Big Dad good-bye?"

She felt hard inside, like an old bucket empty of paint. The hardness translated itself into a scowl. "I don't feel like it," she said, refusing to look at them.

She waited for him to make her, but he didn't. Then she felt worse. It wasn't Dad's fault that everything was so terrible today. He hadn't done anything to upset her. He had, in fact, bent over backwards to accommodate her feelings. But now she had gone so far into the hardness she did not know how to turn back. If she could go to sleep in a box and wake up in another place tomorrow, maybe then she would be all right.

DorJo came around to the other side of the car, opened the door, and got in the back. Arden felt a pang at realizing she had left DorJo to fend for herself there at the last. Her face, too, was closed. They might as well have been in different countries, although they were only inches apart.

"Maybe we'll be seeing you in a couple of weeks," Dad said to Gran and Big Dad as he got into the car. "Remember, give

Hill responsibility. He's good at it—he can haul his share of the weight."

"He'll be fine." Big Dad's rumbly voice was comforting. He patted Dad's arm. "We're grateful to you for letting him come here. I know it's not easy."

Dad gave him a one-sided smile and started the engine. As they backed out of the driveway, Arden risked a look. Her grandparents stood side by side, waving. Upstairs, at the front window, she imagined she saw Hill's dim figure looking down at them.

CHAPTER 17

THE SILENCE DURING THE HOMEWARD TRIP WAS SUFFOCATING. The afternoon sun slanted through the rear window and warmed Arden's neck, but the warmth did not penetrate the darkness inside her. She knew now just how much she had counted on the fun they were going to have that day in Grierson to soften DorJo's anger when she learned that her mother had been looking for her. For the first time since she could remember, going back to Haverlee offered Arden no comfort. What awaited her was as bad as what she had just left.

Supposing she told DorJo right now about yesterday? She played out the scene in her mind.

ARDEN: *DorJo, I have something to tell you and you're not going to like it.*
DORJO: (turning slowly and locking eyes) *What?*
ARDEN: *Your mother came to our house yesterday afternoon while you were upstairs. She was looking for you. I acted like I didn't know where you were . . .*

186

After that the scenario blurred somewhat. DorJo would leap at her and hold her down, yelling at her to tell everything. And after she had done so, DorJo would give her a look of contempt so profound that Arden would have to shut her eyes to blot it out.

Or DorJo would just sit there and shake her head in disbelief, saying nothing. The contempt would be the same, though, no matter what came before. That's what happened when a person betrayed a best friend.

And, of course, Dad would be hearing about it for the first time, too. He might be calmer than DorJo, but he would be angry.

No, she couldn't say it here. But it kept her from saying anything else, too, such as how sorry she was for trying to make DorJo like only the things she herself liked about Grierson. It had never occurred to her that DorJo might like the city and would want to explore it. She was sorry for not taking more pains to help Gran and DorJo get to know each other. Now Dor would think Gran was stuck up when she really wasn't.

"Would you girls like to stop for a snack?" Dad asked. "We're almost to Layson."

"I guess so," Arden said, thinking that it would provide a few minutes' delay, for whatever good that would do. "What about you, Dor?"

"Doesn't matter. Whatever you want to do."

They pulled in at a McDonald's and ordered drinks and fries. They sat at one of the little rectangular tables and avoided each other's eyes the entire time, speaking in monosyllables mostly about things none of them cared about. Arden wished Mom was along. Even when Mom was mad or sad, she made good conversation. Dad was good about it so long as he wasn't down himself, but today he wasn't pretending that leaving Hill in Grierson didn't bother him. She wished she could cheer him up.

When they got back into the car, Arden made a stab at conversation with DorJo. "It'll still be daylight when we get back. What do you say we go to Seth's for a little while?"

"I don't want to."

"But I don't want to go without you."

"Look, Arden," said DorJo, folding her arms impatiently, "we don't have to do every single thing together, do we?"

"No, of course not." But, she wanted to say, that wasn't the point. They were already so far apart that unless they did *something* together soon, the rift wouldn't be fixable.

It seemed forever before they approached Haverlee. Arden looked out of the window as they passed the fields on the outskirts of town, the City Limits sign, the modest houses.

"Ahhhh!" Dad sighed. "Home, to the Great Metropolis!"

"You don't have to make fun of it!" Arden said sharply.

"Excuse *me*," he said, and let the matter go. Arden felt even guiltier. Every time she opened her mouth, she made someone feel bad.

"You don't want to go to walk or something?" she asked DorJo again as they climbed out of the car.

"No."

Discouraged, Arden followed DorJo into the house. She knew Dad was looking at them, although he didn't say anything.

Inside, the house was superclean and shining. Rich smells of beef stew filled the air. Dad headed for the kitchen to find Mom. DorJo went straight upstairs without a word and without looking back. Arden stood alone in the front hall, feeling sorry for herself and a little frightened. The room she shared with DorJo wasn't big enough to hold both of them while they were on the outs. Dad and Mom were probably commiserating about Hill, so that barging into the kitchen would be an intrusion. It was awful not to have a place, especially when she needed to think.

She solved the problem by locking herself in the downstairs bathroom. She knelt on the toilet seat and looked out of the little window overlooking the backyard. She even entertained notions of climbing out and running away somewhere, maybe to the hideout. They'd think she was still in the bathroom even after she was long gone. But there was a big, bristly bush right under the window. The exit would be too painful. Her Timex ticked loudly in the silence. She told herself to quit acting like a little kid.

She unlocked the door and opened it, listening to see if she could tell from the sounds where everyone was.

"Arden?" Mom called from the kitchen. "Come here a sec."

Relieved, she hurried to the kitchen. Dad had gone outside. Arden could see him through the window hauling a bulging plastic trash bag, probably the remains of Mom's housecleaning. Mom reached out with the arm she wasn't using to stir the stew and hugged her close for a moment. "How was the day?"

For about two seconds Arden considered saying, "Fine." But suddenly everything that had been stuck inside her began to come loose. It was the effect that Mom had on her.

"Bad." She gazed at the steam rising from the bubbling pot.

"Oh? What happened?"

Arden wondered where to begin. She opened her mouth, but she had the strange feeling that no matter what she told, it wouldn't be the whole truth. In spite of all there was to tell, she closed her mouth and looked at Mom helplessly.

"I don't know." It seemed to be the most honest thing she could say.

"Well, a lot of change has happened in the past couple of

weeks," Mom said. "It's bound to be confusing."

Arden nodded, but somehow "confusing" didn't seem adequate to explain the great quakes and surges she'd been through.

"Here—take over the stew-stirring while I get the salad ready, please. I put some thickening in and I don't want it to stick." Mom handed her the large metal spoon and Arden moved it back and forth in the roiling broth. It felt good to have something to do.

"Where's DorJo?" Mom asked.

"Upstairs. She's mad . . . I think." Now that she said it, she wasn't sure she was right. DorJo didn't seem angry, just closed up.

"Do you know why?"

Arden told about DorJo not wanting to play with the stuff in the attic junk room, and about going to sleep in the glider, and how DorJo had walked by herself all the way to the center of town and back.

"Wow! That was brave of her!" Mom exclaimed.

"Yes, but she got back late for dinner."

"Oh," said Mom in a quieter voice. She knew how Gran liked for everyone to be on time for meals.

"I made it worse because I fussed at her. I wanted her to make a good impression on Gran, especially after she said Gran didn't like her." She looked at Mom, ashamed. "That's pretty awful, isn't it?"

"Well, in an unfamiliar place like that, it would have been good to stick by her—to make her feel welcome."

"I wish I was in a hole covered up," Arden mumbled, turning back to the stew.

"What? I couldn't hear you."

"It's not important."

"Seth Fox came by this morning to see if you two wanted

to go skating at his uncle's rollerskating rink in Porterfield. I told him perhaps you'd see him tomorrow."

Funny, thought Arden. A week ago, an invitation to the Porterfield rink would have been exciting. Today she felt nothing.

"Is there something you need to tell me?" Mom asked suddenly.

"About what?" Arden tried to make her tone nonchalant.

"We had another visitor today besides Seth."

Arden didn't look at Mom. She stirred and stirred the stew, watching it burp and bubble and roll. "Mrs. Huggins?" she said finally.

"Yes. She told me she came over yesterday afternoon."

Seconds passed. Arden could feel her skin prickle from perspiration. Her clothes were suddenly too warm. "What did you say to her?"

"I said I hadn't known—that you didn't tell anyone. That's true, isn't it—that you didn't tell anyone, not even DorJo?"

Arden nodded.

"Why didn't you?"

This was what walking on a tightrope over a canyon must feel like. "Because it would have messed up everything we planned, and I thought it wouldn't be fair to Hill or to you and Dad for us to have a big ruckus on Hill's last night home. And it would upset DorJo—she'd go home. So I just decided not to tell until we got back today."

"That was a pretty big decision for you to make by yourself, wasn't it?"

"Yes'm. I guess it was."

"Arden, Mrs. Huggins was almost hysterical. It took two hours of continuous talking to get her calmed down. What if I hadn't stayed home today?"

Arden screwed up her courage enough to put down the

spoon and face Mom. Her eyes burned. "I thought about it both ways. I knew if I told anyone, we'd have to do something about it right then. Mrs. Huggins has had days and days to look for DorJo. I figured one more day wouldn't make that much difference."

Mom looked at her closely, a slight furrow between her eyebrows. "But Arden—this is really serious business."

"O.K. So I made the wrong choice!" she burst out. "I'm sorry! I should've told Mrs. Huggins the minute I opened the door: 'DorJo's upstairs—go up there and haul her down!' "

"No," Mom said patiently. "You couldn't take that responsibility. But you should have told your dad and me as soon as we got home from work yesterday."

Arden turned back to the stew, looking at it through a blur of tears. "What happened?"

"I was cleaning—running the vacuum," said Mom. "It's a wonder I heard the doorbell, but it happened to chime when I was right under the bell box upstairs. I came down and there she was, upset and scared but not willing to go to the sheriff. After I asked her inside, it took a while for me to finally piece together what happened yesterday. She said she came here to ask if you knew where DorJo was, and you told her no, but that she should come back later when your Dad and I were home."

"That's not right," Arden broke in. "I never told her I didn't know. She didn't come right out and ask me that."

"But you did tell her to come back, even though you knew we wouldn't be here."

"I wasn't thinking. I just wanted her to go away before DorJo found out she was here. She told me she probably wouldn't come back."

"But she did, around seven. She says she waited an hour

or so on the porch and then went home. By that time she was very upset "

Arden was astonished that what she had imagined last night was real. It gave her an eerie feeling. Had she made it happen merely by thinking about it?

"I told her I was sorry," Mom went on. "I told her that DorJo had been with us for a number of days, that she was frightened to go back home. I said DorJo feared she would be sent away for what she had done. Mrs. Huggins acted surprised that DorJo told us about the scene between them—and ashamed, too. She admitted she'd let her temper get the best of her. She wants DorJo to come home."

Indignation stirred in Arden. "I'll bet she didn't make any promises about treating DorJo like a person for a change, did she?"

"No," said Mom. "She's not obliged to make promises to us."

"Jessie doesn't believe their mother will ever be different," Arden said. "Jessie doesn't *want* DorJo to go back home."

Mom sat down in one of the chairs and leaned her elbows on the table. "You know something, Arden? I'll bet if Mrs. Huggins had some other people in town to give her support and friendship, she'd make an extra effort to be responsible."

Arden turned the idea over in her mind. It was true she had never heard DorJo mention any particular friends her mother had.

"I don't know," she said. "She doesn't seem like the kind of person you could get close to. She's tough."

"You have to be tough if you think nobody cares whether you live or die," Mom said. "But she knows that we care about DorJo and Jessie. She has too much pride to let us outdo her in that department."

"You didn't tell her where Jessie was, did you?"

"Of course not—I didn't have permission." Mom got up and went back to her salad-making.

"Did you tell her you'd make DorJo go home?"

"No. I told Mrs. Huggins that when you folks got back from Grierson we'd talk it over. I said it would be up to DorJo to decide."

"I'll bet she yelled about that," said Arden. "She probably said DorJo didn't have the sense or the right to decide."

"Actually, she just acted kind of sad. I think she believes neither of the girls will want to go back."

"DorJo would," said Arden morosely. "She's so softhearted where her mother is concerned."

"Would you do that?" Mom asked. "I mean, if I'd treated you and Hill that way, would you give me another chance?"

Arden turned quickly, caught off guard by the question. Mom stood there with her salady hands drooping damply from the wrist and a serious look on her face.

"Well, sure I would, for *you!*" Arden said righteously. She was going to add, "But you're different," only somehow it occurred to her between one word and the next that maybe from DorJo's point of view there wasn't all that much difference. Your mom is your mom. She smiled sheepishly.

Mom smiled back and put her hands back in the salad bowl. "Boy, that's a relief!" she said. "A person never knows when she might take a wrong turn . . ."

"I guess I have to tell DorJo, huh?" Arden said in a small voice.

Mom was sympathetic. "Yes. The sooner, the better."

"You mean, before dinner? How about if you come with me?" Then she saw Mom's look and said, "Well, maybe I'll do it myself."

Dad came in the back door just then, dusting his hands

together. "Woman, you really bulldozed this place today! I haven't seen that much trash since we moved here twelve years ago."

"Sometimes that's what it takes," Mom said. "Now if we move anytime soon, I won't have nearly so much to do."

Dad peered over at Arden. She could tell by his expression that he knew about Mrs. Huggins and was waiting for her to say something. She mustered all her effort and looked him in the eye.

"I'm getting ready to go talk to DorJo right now."

Dad put his arm across her shoulders and gave her a quick squeeze. "It'll turn out O.K., Bird. Don't worry."

CHAPTER 18

EASY FOR HIM TO SAY, SHE THOUGHT A FEW MINUTES LATER, as she stood at the bottom of the stairs. It was awfully quiet up there. She marched up, counting each step, so she wouldn't have to think about what she was going to say. Her feet thudded on the carpeting. She hoped DorJo would hear her coming and get ready.

But when she opened the bedroom door and looked in, DorJo was sitting on the window seat looking out at the back-yard. She was as still as a statue. The afternoon light made her skin look like smooth, white marble.

Arden came on into the room and sat down on her own bed. "Dor, can we talk?"

"Go ahead." DorJo's voice seemed to come from some other part of the room. She wouldn't turn her head to look at Arden.

Here it was, and she was no more prepared than when she had begun to dread it a whole day ago. She swallowed and plunged in.

"Well, I've got a lot to tell. You are going to be mad, but

I hope you'll listen to the whole thing. I'm going to tell you why I . . . did what I did."

DorJo shifted her position so that she could see Arden, drawing her legs up slowly as though she had no energy. "Hurry up," she said.

"Yesterday . . . after we came home from school and you were up here? Well . . . your mother came to our house looking for you."

DorJo sat up instantly. Her mouth formed an O, the beginning of a question.

"Now, wait—" Arden held up her hand. "Wait until I tell the whole thing. I was scared to tell her you were here. I didn't tell her you *weren't* because she didn't ask me that, but I . . . she left thinking I didn't know where you were."

DorJo made a little choking noise. Arden talked faster.

"I told her she should come back when Mom and Dad were home. She said she probably wouldn't, but as it turns out, she did. She came back last night while we were in Porterfield. Then . . . Mom says she came back today, while we were gone."

"Was she mad? Was she trying to get me arrested?" DorJo was breathless.

Arden shook her head. This was the hardest part. "No. She was worried about you."

"How could you not tell me that!" DorJo's shriek rang in the room. She was on her feet now, moving toward Arden. Her eyes were slits. "How could we be side by side all this time and you not *tell* me?"

"I didn't tell anybody."

"But *why*?" It was a wail. "What right did you have not to tell!"

"No right," she mumbled. "But I'll try to tell you why, if you'll listen."

DorJo turned on her heel and walked away. "I'm listening."

Arden tried to explain her decision to keep it a secret because it would spoil the family's plans for the evening. Even as she spoke, though, she thought it was a puny-sounding excuse. "Last night I thought it was up to me to keep everything all pleasant and happy by not telling anybody your mother had come here," she finished lamely.

"But it would've made *me* happy!" DorJo exclaimed. "She came *looking* for me, Arden. She was worried. I could've gone with her!"

Arden felt about three inches tall. "I wasn't thinking about it that way," she muttered. "I thought we'd have so much fun in Grierson today that when I finally did tell, you wouldn't be so mad at me."

"And when was that going to be?" DorJo said with scorn. "Next July?"

"No. Tonight. I'm really sorry, Dor—it's the worst mistake I ever made."

"I'm tired of this!" DorJo's eyes were dry and hard. "I'm getting out of here. Going home, where I belong." She went over to the drawer where her clean clothes were neatly folded and yanked it open. She took out the clothes she had worn the day she came to the Giffords from hiding in the woods. With her back turned to Arden, she unbuttoned the blue shirt Mom had bought and flung it off. Over her head she slipped the white knit shirt. Next she removed the new jeans and pulled on her old ones. The torn tennis shoes were next. She did all of this rapidly but with great deliberation. Finally she picked up the cast-off clothes from the floor, folded them, and put them on the bed. "I'm sorry your mom spent all that money on me. I'll pay her back."

"Those are yours," said Arden. "You take them."

"No. Y'all can give them to the Good Will." DorJo moved

toward the door. Arden jumped up and stood in her way She felt so strange. They'd never had this kind of conflict before, one that might actually lead to physical struggle. She had no doubts about who would be the winner.

"Wait a minute," she said, with a firmness she didn't feel. "You can't just walk out of here without telling my folks— *they* didn't know either—"

DorJo shoved her aside then, not roughly, but Arden knew for the first time why those of her classmates who tended toward hand-to-hand combat in settling arguments had such respect for her. In another second the door slammed behind her, and Arden was left with the echo resounding in her ears.

She recovered quickly, yanking the door open and following at DorJo's heels along the hall and down the stairs. Just as they reached the bottom step, Mom came out into the hall.

"Stew's ready, girls. We're eating in the kitchen tonight."

DorJo stopped. Arden, in close pursuit, came to a screeching halt, narrowly avoiding a collision. Neither of them said a word, but Arden tried to signal to Mom with her eyes that there was trouble.

"What's up?" Mom asked, looking at DorJo.

"I'm leaving," said DorJo. "I'm going home."

"Right this minute?" Mom asked.

"Yes'm. And I don't want anybody to try and stop me." The defiant words did not match DorJo's respectful manner.

"All right," Mom said as if it were the most reasonable statement anyone could make. "But I've already served the stew. You might as well take twenty extra minutes to eat. Your mother may not have anything fixed, since she doesn't know you're coming."

DorJo hesitated. "Oh, well . . . all right," she said finally. Mom's practical nature was hard to argue with. "But I don't want anybody telling me I shouldn't go. I'll eat, then I'll leave.

If y'all start in about it, I'm just gonna leave sooner."

"Fair enough," said Mom. "Do you mind if I tell Tom?"

"Never mind," said Dad's voice from the doorway. "I heard it."

It was certainly a strange meal. Everyone was quiet. The electric rooster clock swung its second hand around and around. Nearly five minutes passed with no one saying a word other than "Thank you" or "Pass the salad dressing."

We're under a spell, Arden thought, concentrating on her beef stew. A wicked witch has waved her wand over this house and has drawn all the important words out of our heads. She has collected them in a black bag that she wears around her neck, and she intends to fly on her broom out over the ocean and fling the bag as far as it will go. After that, we'll never again be able to talk real—it will always be chitchat or silence.

"I don't want you to think I don't 'preciate what you've done for me," DorJo said suddenly. Mom sat up straighter. Dad put his spoon on his plate. Arden kept eating, her eyes riveted on DorJo.

"You have been real nice," she went on, "but this ain't where I belong. I'll feel a whole lot better when I'm back home with Mama."

"What's going to happen when she starts yelling at you again?" Arden asked. "And when she starts reminding you about the knife?"

"Arden!" Mom warned.

"I've thought about that," DorJo said calmly. "Before, I was so scared she'd go away and leave us again that I'd take anything she said. I'm not gonna pretend anymore. I'll speak up when I have to. It's holding all that stuff in for too long that makes me lose my temper."

There was a little silence, and then Dad said, "That sounds wise. I would think your mother could respect that."

200

"She and I had a long talk today," Mom told DorJo. "At first she was pretty angry—she felt deceived by all of us."

Arden looked down at the stew, afraid to meet DorJo's eyes.

"But I tried to explain to her how frightened you were," Mom continued, "not just because she had threatened to have you arrested, but because you had lost your temper and felt out of control. I think she hadn't seen things from your point of view. She really does want you to come home. I believe she means to try to be more . . . constant."

DorJo's smile was almost too bright to behold. Arden's throat ached.

"I'm glad Mama and you had a chance to talk," DorJo said shyly. "So you'd see she's not that bad. I 'preciate you explaining to her why I ran off and stayed—I don't know if I could've done it so she'd understand."

"Well," said Mom, taking a deep breath and looking around the table at them, "all's well that end's well, to borrow a phrase—right?"

"It's certainly an improvement," Dad commented.

Yes, thought Arden, smiling for DorJo's sake. But why was it so hard to improve everything at once? Things would be better between DorJo and her mother, but now they were worse between DorJo and Arden. She did not know what she could do to make DorJo trust her again.

"As soon as we finish, we'll walk over with you," said Mom.

DorJo shook her head emphatically. "No ma'am—I want to go by myself!"

"I don't mean we'd go all the way to the door with you," Mom said. "I'd like for us to be near enough to make sure you actually go into the house. We'll stand where your mother can't see us. If—for any reason—you can't go in, then we'll help you decide what to do next. I will *not* let you spend any more nights in the woods—it's October. Either you'll have to come back here, or we'll take you to Granpa Huggins."

DorJo appeared to turn this over in her mind. "Well," she said finally, "there's no need of it, but I guess that'll be all right."

"I could put the new clothes in a bag for you," Arden said, thinking that by now DorJo might have changed her mind.

"No. Maybe I'll come back for 'em some day later on. I don't want Mama to feel bad, me coming in with a bunch of stuff she couldn't've bought for me."

"Well, let's hurry and finish here," Mom said briskly, "so we can get home before dark."

For everyone in the room but Arden, it was already as good as done.

When the four of them started toward DorJo's house, the sun was just disappearing behind the trees. Its orange edge, like the rim of a giant penny, grew narrower and narrower and then was gone. The early October chill made Arden shiver. DorJo's summer shirt was no protection, but she did not appear to be cold.

The girls walked side by side, while Dad and Mom followed a few feet behind. For Arden it was like a walk to the gallows, or like boarding a plane with a one-way ticket.

"Are you still mad at me?" she asked softly.

DorJo didn't answer right away. Then she said, "Mixed up is more like it. I don't know how you could've fooled me like that, but I guess I'll get over it."

"I'll never do it again," Arden said miserably but as she spoke she wondered whether she and DorJo would ever be close enough again for it to matter.

In a minute or two Dad reached out and put his hand on Arden's shoulder. "Maybe we should stop here, Bird. The bushes will be a shield."

DorJo pressed her lips together and took a deep breath. She

wiped her hands on the back of her jeans, then she turned to them. "Thank y'all again. I won't forget how good you've been to me. And I'll see you at school on Monday," she said to Arden.

"Not before that?" Arden asked.

"I don't know. Maybe." Then she moved swiftly across the yard toward the little house.

Arden was glad the light was fading. She stared unblinking as DorJo climbed the rickety steps and knocked on the door. DorJo said something, but the distance made it impossible for them to hear. The moment was suspended, a story with two endings. A person could look ahead and see DorJo going inside, or turning and coming back down the steps, but there was no way to know before it happened which ending it would be.

Abruptly the screen door opened, and in the next second DorJo disappeared inside. The door closed behind her.

CHAPTER 19

NEXT MORNING ARDEN ATE BREAKFAST AND CONTEMPLATED THE blank space across the table where Hill always sat. Mom and Dad were in their accustomed places, but somehow the three of them were not enough to surround the table, either with bodies or conversation. And of course it wasn't just Hill's absence, but DorJo's as well. Three was a lot fewer than five.

"I miss Hill," Mom said aloud what they were all thinking. "I keep opening my mouth to ask you to go wake him up, Arden, and then I remember he's not here."

Dad reached over and squeezed Mom's hand. "Yes. I've been counting us. With one gone, I feel like a three-legged mule."

Well, thought Arden, making tracks in her oatmeal with her spoon, I guess that makes me a two-legged mule. She wondered how a two-legged mule would get around, and decided it was impossible unless it was missing the two back legs and had a little cart to rest its hind end on. Any other combination of missing legs made moving out of the question.

"What're you thinking, Bird?" Dad asked.

"About two-legged mules," she said, defying him with her eyes to ask any further questions.

He nodded, knowing right away what she meant. She was grateful to have a dad who didn't have to have everything explained.

Going to church helped Arden keep her mind off the sudden emptiness of her life. But in another way it only made matters worse. People asked about Hill. Had he really moved to Grierson? Didn't he like Haverlee? Would he come back for holidays? She got tired of answering questions. She struggled to make the answers fair when what she really wanted to say was I don't know why he had to leave! I think he made a mistake, going off to that noisy place! On the other hand, she didn't like the implication in some of the questions that Hill was stuck-up—that Haverlee wasn't good enough for him. She added a little creative twist of her own, to the effect that Gran and Big Dad were getting older, so they needed someone like Hill around to help them out. She made it sound like an unselfish act on the part of the family, lending him out like that. She did not, however, say this around Mom and Dad.

"You want to go over to Porterfield for lunch?" Dad asked as they were driving home after services. "We could be back by two."

"Not really," said Mom. She leaned over and rested her head on Dad's shoulder. From her place in the backseat Arden got one of those sudden lumps in her throat. She didn't have anyone, not to fight with or to lean on. The seat seemed very wide and empty.

"Do you have big plans for this afternoon, Bird?" Dad asked.

"Sort of," she hedged. But don't ask me what, she added to herself. He didn't.

They ate leftover stew and sandwiches, then Mom and Dad

divided the thick Sunday newspaper between them and settled in the living room to read. Arden went upstairs and walked around. The silence of the place was oppressive. Hill's room was as bare as picked bones, the bathroom empty and cleaner than it had been in months. Her own room seemed too large now that she was once again the only occupant. She wandered over and opened the closet. DorJo's new clothes hanging there didn't help. She briefly considered gathering up the clothes in a neat bundle and taking them to DorJo, mostly for an excuse to go over there. But then maybe DorJo would think Arden wanted to get rid of anything that belonged to her. She sighed and closed the closet door. In some situations you couldn't win for losing.

It was only one thirty. The afternoon stretched ahead interminably. She longed for something that would take up all her attention, something that would exchange all thinking for doing, like playing when she was a little kid. The problem was, she couldn't imagine what it would be. She had never had that problem in her younger days. Maybe, she thought mournfully, this was a sign she was beginning to turn into a teenager!

"Well," she scolded herself, "staying around here isn't going to help!" She dug a pair of jeans and a shirt from the drawer and changed clothes. After putting on her sneakers, she had a sudden inspiration. Back she went to Hill's room to check the chest of drawers. There, sure enough, were a couple of sweatshirts he had decided not to take to Grierson. She picked the navy one with HAVERLEE HIGH SCHOOL in white letters across the front and pulled it on over her shirt. It was pretty large, she had to admit, as she looked at herself in his mirror, but that was the style. She pushed the sleeves up halfway to her elbows so the cuffs wouldn't hang over her hands, and then tiptoed downstairs.

"I'm going out!" she called in the direction of the living room, then slipped through the front door and closed it quickly behind her before Mom or Dad could ask where she was going.

She walked southward with a purposeful stride, even though she hadn't the vaguest notion where she'd end up. If she looked like she was going somewhere people wouldn't stop her. Haverlee certainly was an empty-looking place on Sunday afternoon. After a few minutes she slowed her pace. The great oaks and maples lining the street caught the sunlight and filtered it downward through multicolored leaves. High above, the breeze moved the branches back and forth with an insistent whisper. The ache in her chest began to ease a little.

Maybe I'll drop by Seth's, she thought, trying the idea for size. She thought about his damaged heart, and about the model cars that took up every available surface in his room. He would be very glad for her to drop by on a dull Sunday afternoon. Maybe he'd let her try to put together one of his new models.

But as soon as she approached, she knew that no one was home. The modest little white house, all tucked about with bright fall flowers like a prim lady, appeared ready to receive callers, but no cars were around and the blinds were drawn. She went up on the porch and knocked. When no one came to the door she went around to the backyard. There was the placid pond where the three of them had poled the raft. It seemed like a hundred years ago instead of only a few days. Disconsolate, she kicked at a grass clump and turned away.

She meant to go home, but when she reached her own street, she couldn't bear the thought of going back to the quiet, echoing house. She turned abruptly up another lane. Before long she found she was heading toward the clay bluffs and the hideout.

On the day that she had gone there looking for DorJo, its

loneliness had almost overwhelmed her. Now, however, she needed a place to be alone. The ache in her chest had intensified.

For the first time since DorJo showed her the hideout, Arden was careless about getting there. A part of her felt indifferent. She and DorJo would never go there again as pals—something was broken between them.

She took the most direct route and reached the woods in about half the time it took ordinarily. A good thing, too, she thought as she clambered through the scrub and underbrush toward the clay bluff. I'm going to be blubbering in about three minutes.

She pushed aside the kudzu and pulled herself thankfully into the waiting niche. For a few seconds she sat at the edge, dangling her feet and catching her breath. She surveyed the path she had taken and decided that it wasn't so noticeable, even though she had been careless. Maybe all these months they had been careful for nothing.

Arden drew her legs up and sat cross-legged as she and DorJo had done so often. She pulled the kudzu curtain back in place so she could no longer see out. The sock she had left as a mute message to DorJo lay there undisturbed across the two yellow plastic cups. Beside them sat the can of Vienna sausages, the water jar, and the box of raisins. The cave was as still and deserted as a vacant warehouse, but she imagined ghostly echoes of the good times she and DorJo had had in it.

The tears began then, simply welling up and streaming down her face. She rocked back and forth, not making a sound. It was a strange sort of weeping, almost like drowning. Usually when she cried she was angry, or had hurt feelings, or was physically in pain. She made a lot of noise then. This time, though, the tears were an overflow of deep sadness. Maybe when they'd run long enough she'd get to a dryer part and the noise would begin. She didn't even bother to get out the one ratty Kleenex in her jeans pocket.

After what seemed a very long time, when in spite of the pine-straw carpet her backside had begun to hurt from sitting on the clay floor, she blew her nose on the sock and then wiped her face on the sleeve of Hill's sweatshirt. It smelled clean and fresh, like the sun and air in which it had hung to dry. Haverlee air. She looked around the cave once more, memorizing it. She took one of the bits of colored glass as a souvenir. The two plastic cups mocked her with their smug togetherness. Well, she would let them stay there, maybe for the same reason people put tombstones on graves.

When she heard the noise outside she thought at first it was an animal of some sort—a rabbit perhaps, or a stray dog. But then she realized it made more fuss than a whole passel of rabbits. Right away she regretted her lack of care in coming to the hideout. Someone had discovered her tracks and had followed her. She certainly hoped it wasn't Albert Twiggs, especially since DorJo wasn't around. She wasn't scared of Albert exactly, but she wasn't sure what he'd do to get revenge for his humiliation that day at the creek.

She sat scarcely breathing. The noise stopped. She began to feel a little afraid. Supposing it wasn't Albert Twiggs or anyone else she knew? Suppose it was an absolute stranger, passing through Haverlee on the way to some other town?

When the kudzu curtain was suddenly pushed aside, she gave a little involuntary scream.

"I thought this is where you'd be!" DorJo said jubilantly. "I been looking for you the whole blessed afternoon, up one street and down the other. Your folks said you went out and didn't say where you were going. Move over—I'm climbing up."

She said it all in almost one breath. Then she stopped and looked hard at the openmouthed Arden. "I *can* come up, can't I?"

Arden recovered her senses and grabbed DorJo's arm. "What do you mean, can you come up? You ninny—get in here, quick! I've been waiting and waiting. How could you have walked up one street and down the other without finding me? I was doing the same thing!" And they fell into a fit of hysterical laughter at the thought of themselves just missing each other, like mice in a maze.

They talked and talked through the afternoon. They ate the Vienna sausages and the raisins.

"Is it different?" Arden asked cautiously. "At your house, I mean?"

"Yeah, some. Mama yells sometimes, but I think she really is trying to do better. The main thing that's different is me— how I feel. I'm not . . . scared."

"Do you think she's going to stay this time?"

DorJo shrugged. "She talks like it. She's going to go see Mr. Cranston tomorrow about getting a job at the school cafeteria. That way she can be home in the afternoons and at night."

"That would be good." Arden nodded. "I hope she does it. But what about Jessie? Will she come back, too?"

DorJo looked thoughtful. "Well, this morning Mama and I went over to Granpa's."

Arden's eyes got big. She had visions of a screaming, shouting free-for-all with accusations flying back and forth and not much good coming from it. "You mean—you just went over there without—I mean, what did they do?"

"Jessie was mad at me," DorJo admitted. "She said I didn't have a right to take Mama there without asking Granpa first. But Granpa didn't mind. Mama said over and over how sorry she was, and how she wanted to make up for being so unresponsible. Jessie huffed off upstairs and wouldn't talk to her, but Granpa said to let Jessie stay on with him for a while, until she cooled down. Then he would talk to her about it. I guess that's how it'll be." She sighed. "I don't want Jessie to stay mad. I want us all to be together."

Arden was very glad that DorJo had something to hope for and that her wish seemed to be coming true. But at the same time the new brightness in DorJo's life only served as a contrast to the way her own life had shrunk and dimmed. It was as though some wizard had turned their lives topsy-turvy, granting to DorJo what had once belonged to Arden. Perhaps that was the nature of magic kingdoms, though—their kings and queens were forever being deposed and exiled for a time, until they had lived through some ordeal, or had accomplished certain tasks.

"The main thing I need to say," said DorJo, turning to face her, "is that I'm sorry for the way I have acted to you ever since Friday. Jessie mixed me up so, and then the trip to your folks' house in Grierson was . . . I don't know. I have just acted like a sourpuss, all the way around."

"It was really *my* fault," Arden told her. "I didn't tell you that your mama was looking for you and that made everything so awful. I wouldn't blame you if you never trusted me again."

"Well, maybe it was both of us," DorJo conceded. "That don't matter. What matters is us still being friends . . . if you want to."

Arden smiled slowly, feeling warmth in the region of her heart lifting the heavy bleakness and pushing it away.

"If I want to? Dumb question!" she managed to say. "Everybody knows a three-legged mule gets around a whole lot better than a two-legged one."

"What?" DorJo frowned, puzzled.

"Nothing—it's just a joke." Arden got to her knees and

dusted the seat of her jeans. "Come on—let's go see if Seth's back from wherever he went. Maybe we can get him to give us another invitation to his uncle's skating rink in Porterfield."

DorJo climbed down first. Arden took the bit of colored glass out of her pocket and laid it on the ledge again, beside the others. The yellow cups did not look so smug anymore. With a grin, she followed DorJo over the ledge and helped pull the branch-and-kudzu camouflage across the entrance. Surely, after all, they would be back.